MW01002067

FORGET
you not

HARLOE RAE

Forget You Not
Copyright © 2017 by Harloe Rae
All rights reserved.

This is a work of fiction and any resemblance to persons, names, characters, places, brands, media, and incidents are either the product of the author's imagination or purely coincidental.

Cover Design:
Talia's Book Covers

Editing:
Ace Gray

Interior Design & Formatting:
Christine Borgford, Type A Formatting

This book is dedicated to
my very own Prince Charming.
My husband restored my faith and belief
in happily ever after and all the other
love-fest, gooey goodness. He's *the one!*

Lark is close to my heart and
her story is very special to me.
I hope she speaks to you as well.
Plus, Rowen is magical. You'll see . . .

PROLOGUE

Lark

Seven years earlier . . .

Working at a restaurant sucks sometimes. Like right now. *Why is it so slow?*

Usually Friday afternoons bring in a decent lunch crowd but that's definitely not the case today. The other host got cut an hour ago after we finished rolling two full bins of silverware. I've been stuck at the front alone ever since, trying to keep myself preoccupied by doodling in my notepad while desperately hoping a customer strolls in. I'd even accept the overly chatty manager from the bank across the street at this rate.

Just as I'm starting to draw another cartoon heart, the outer door swings open and a relieved sigh whooshes from me. I toss my pen aside and slide the decorated paper into my apron. When my focus returns to the person coming in, my breath stalls in my lungs.

I'd usually have a polite smile plastered across my face as I rushed forward to greet the guests but my entire body is frozen solid due to the stunning sight before me. Tingles erupt along my skin as my heart takes off in a sprint, but I still can't move.

The most gorgeous man I've ever seen is only a few feet away and my stomach nervously tangles in a complicated twist. He's tall and broad, easily over six feet, which swallows up my petite frame. Probably a few years older than me, this guy still has a hint of youth lighting up his smooth features. My pulse skyrockets as I get trapped in his swirling ocean irises that remind me of a tropical paradise. I remain suspended in my paralyzed state as he approaches the host stand with a confident stride.

Wow, he's beautiful.

My cheeks heat with that thought and I dip my head to hide the flush covering my face. I attempt a sneaky peek by glancing up at him through my lowered lashes. When my gaze connects with his, I notice a sexy smirk lifting his lips and it tightens my chest further.

Crap, I'm totally busted.

I clear my parched throat so I can properly greet him before getting fired for gawking, but he beats me to it.

"Hey." He pauses with an audible swallow and I watch his Adam's apple bob. A soft chuckle rises from him as he rubs over his left pec. "Wow, you're really beautiful. Is that weird for me to say? *Shit.*" His feet shuffle nervously as his gaze lowers to the floor before quickly focusing on me again. "I feel really creepy blurting it out but that's the truth. Sorry if I'm being super awkward. I don't know what's wrong with me. Tell me to stop talking." He laughs again before sucking in a deep breath. "What's your name?" His voice is like melted chocolate filling my hungry stomach. His extremely good looks match the silky-smooth timbre that's thrumming my bones. He seems anxious, which makes my heart race even faster.

As I continue silently staring at him, I determine he's my every teenage fantasy come to life and reminds me of Ryan Gosling from *The Notebook*. All striking blue eyes and dark-blond hair that's the perfect length to run your fingers through. That's what I'm talking about.

I do my best to collect my stray thoughts before wiping my sweaty palms on my jeans. I lock my wobbling knees and stand up straight, then raise my chin to meet his burning stare.

"Umm, hello. Thanks for coming to Brack's Box. My name is Lark and I'll be showing you to a table. How many are in your party? Oh, I should have asked if you were dining in or carrying out. Will you be eating here?" I feel like a total idiot as my speech fumbles and bumbles. My tone is shaking worse than my trembling hands. At least he appears flustered too.

The sexy stranger moves closer until he's hovering on the edge of my personal space. His chest seems to shudder as he reaches out and traces a jagged line from my temple to my jaw with a coarse finger. Electric shocks spark along the skin he touched and a small gasp escapes me. I've never had this type of reaction before and it has a hoard of love-struck butterflies taking flight in my belly.

"You're blushing, Lark. Are you nervous too?" His whispered words rush across the small space between us and I shudder in response.

Could I be more embarrassed?

I roll my shoulders back in an effort to infuse my body with strength.

"What? No. No way. Why would you think that? That's just silly." I toss out a lame chuckle—as if he has no effect on me—before taking a step away from him. If my boss came out here and saw me standing so close to a customer, I'd be in serious crap.

This handsome man tilts his head and continues his slow perusal of my face. He lifts a curious brow as a mouth-watering grin stretches his pillowy lips. I'm not sure what to do with myself as his golden glow graces my presence. Everything is a scattered jumble in my brain and I'm not sure what the right move is at the moment. I settle on getting back to work and the task at hand.

"So, do you want a table or are you ordering out?" The line slips out easily enough. Awkward tension skims down my spine as he keeps up with the intense eye contact.

A loud clap of laughter booms out of him.

"Are you trying to get rid of me, Sweetheart?" His white teeth gleam in the overhead lights as a wide smile lifts his cheeks. "I can't seem to stop thinking about how gorgeous your amber eyes are." His breathy pause finds me lost in the kaleidoscope of blue hues that make up his enchanting stare. "My name is Rowen, but all my friends call me Row. It's my pleasure to meet you." He holds out a steady hand for me to shake and I immediately slip my clammy palm into his.

When our skin makes contact again, a blast of fire rushes up my arms until the heat reaches my core. I bite my tongue to trap the moan desperate to escape. His basic touch is lighting me up and shock surges through me. I've read about this type of reaction in romance novels, but this is *actually happening*.

Why does this man have such a powerful impact on my body?

He's turning me into a giggling pile of mush with simple physical connection. My mind is lost to him as well if I'm being totally honest. His expressive gaze appears bottomless and speaks to the lonely spirit within me. The insecurities usually plaguing my mind are forgotten under his attention. My pasty legs and nonexistent curves don't matter to him based off the frantic pulse in his neck.

A low hum yanks me back to reality and I realize Rowen is the one making that delicious noise. Before I can react, he pulls me into his hard body and murmurs close to my ear, "Do you believe in destiny? What about soul mates?"

I can only nod since my mouth feels like desert sand. Could Rowen possibly understand the chaos buzzing in my blood?

His jaw works back and forth. "It seems like I was meant to

come in here today. Does that sound crazy, Lark? I don't know how to describe what's happening to me but you're mixing me all up. This was supposed to be a quick stop but now I never want to leave. Can we sit down, Sweetheart? Maybe eat lunch?"

When a little squeak pushes past my lips and puffs against his neck, a rumble shakes his wide chest that has me leaning further into him.

Unfiltered excitement and overwhelming joy causes my entire body to bloom with intoxicating warmth. *This beautiful guy wants to know more about me.* Shockwaves travel down my spine as my brain whirls in contemplation. I settle on being ambitious and impulsive as my body sways along his.

Screw the consequences.

Rowen's grip tightens slightly and I swear his hands wobble. "I knew you could feel it. Let's go outside where we'll get some privacy." His tone soaks into my thirsty heart but when his request registers into my foggy brain, it seems like a cold bucket of water has been dumped over my head.

What am I doing?!

I suddenly remember where we are, which effectively snaps me out of my romantic haze. I can't believe I'm behaving this way at work. This is definitely not normal—let alone acceptable—and the significant hold this guy already has on me is becoming more obvious.

Breaking contact with him is like ripping off a layer of flesh but it's necessary for now. I'm at my freaking job and need to start acting like it. Once I've placed a few feet between us, air finally travels freely through my lungs and brings fresh clarity to this crazy situation.

The chemistry between us is so powerful that my soul already seems bonded to him, which makes me sound like a whacky person. My fingers comb through my messy brown hair while I try to get a freaking grip on my sanity.

"Alright, pump the brakes for a moment. I can't go anywhere with you now because I'm working. If I don't get back to my job, I won't have one for much longer and I really need the money. How about I find you a nice table outside to eat your lunch and I'll join you once my shift is over. Deal?" I try my best to inject my voice with confidence but I can hear the quiver.

If Rowen notices my fumbling, he's kind enough not to point it out. There is a moment of silence as his stunning ocean eyes sweep along my body from head to toe. Color rises on his flawless face and his fingers fidget nervously.

When his gaze returns to my face, my legs tremble at the raw hunger that's being directed at me. What sounds like a groan pushes past his clenched jaw before he seems to regain control and realizes I'm waiting for confirmation.

"Whatever works for you, Lark. I'll patiently wait hours for even a moment of your time." Rowen sweeps his arm toward the patio door before saying, "Ladies first." I quickly move ahead of him after grabbing a menu.

Once I have him seated and comfortable, I turn to leave but look back for another glimpse at all his yummy sexiness. Rowen shoots me a wink that has me second guessing the devotion to my job.

I'll be off soon enough.

I make my way back inside with an extra spring in my step. Happiness churns in my stomach like gooey caramel. I'm sure this guy is the one I've been waiting for, my rapid heartbeat and clinging urges tell me so. It's never, ever been this way. I might be desperate for love but I'm not going to fall for just anyone. Rowen seems to understand too. His sweeping stare reflected something that reminds me of forever and I'm ready to get lost in his blue waves. He didn't want to leave and I'm sure he never will. I can't wait to share my deepest desires with him.

After a dreadfully dull thirty minutes crawl by, I manage to make my way toward the patio to check on Rowen. As I pass the glass doors and find his table empty, I assume he's in the bathroom or left to grab something real quick.

When a few minutes blend into fifteen and he's still gone, dread begins to spread throughout me like a poison and a weight settles onto my chest.

I try to remain positive and convince myself of his eventual return. Tears blur my vision as a lump forms in my throat but I don't let the sorrow drag me down. At least not yet.

Rowen will be back.

He said there was something special between us.

We're meant to be together.

But we really aren't anything at all.

I never saw Rowen again and the longer he stayed away, the further my fragile heart cracked, until one day there was nothing left to salvage.

ONE

Lark

Now . . .

Want to hear something weird? I'm having a wicked case of Déjà vu.

The type where I can sense I've been in a very specific situation before because it's so freaking familiar. As a tinge of awareness prickles along my scalp and shivers race down my spine, I'm certain something serious is about to go down.

One minute I'm fine, calm as a cucumber as I celebrate Willow and Xander's engagement with a room full of familiar faces. The next, I'm gasping for breath as panic threatens to strangle me.

Are you fucking kidding me right now?!

The illusive man I've been obsessing over since I was seventeen just strolled into the bar. He's been haunting me for seven years and I don't even know his freaking last name. I'm certain of plenty facts though.

I was a girl who believed in finding true love but that vanished up in smoke shortly after this jackass stomped on my naïve heart. Rowen is responsible for starting the downward spiral that caused me to spin out of control while I was desperately trying to find a boy to care about me.

I sound like a complete whack-job.

I'm really not *that* crazy but my mind is currently a jumble of confusion and frustration as everything tilts wildly around me. My knees threaten to buckle and I can't seem to catch my breath. Wayward glances might be directed my way. If these people saw the turmoil that's currently destroying my brain, they'd probably run the other way. Lucky for them, it's all in my head and I'm used to suffering in silence.

There are a few important points to make before this epic disaster unravels any further . . .

I'm well aware of my downfalls, the biggest being my struggle with men. I'll be the first to admit that I have "Daddy-issues". I didn't need my expensive degree in psychology to figure that out.

I grew up without a male role model since my jackass father unexpectedly walked out of my life. He was the first man to rip my heart out and stomp on my overly sensitive feelings. Ever since that catastrophe, I'd been a tad vulnerable when it came to men. At the same time, I became eager to fill the gaping hole his absence created. A desperate girl searching for love never works out well. There were a long line of Prince Charming imposters and huge let downs in my wake.

And the largest one is currently chatting it up with my best friend's fiancé.

What is so wrong with wanting a man to love, honor, and cherish you?

It leads to continuous disappointment and regret.

I was too clingy.

Too demanding.

Too damaged.

Eventually I became too fucking fed up.

My own dad didn't love me enough to stick around so I

shouldn't have been surprised when other guys ran off scared whenever commitment was brought up. Men are a bunch of chicken shits and should come with a fucking warning label.

Don't even bother wasting the time.

I digress . . . Let's return to the original reason I'm melting down and figure out why the *fuck* Rowen is here. An overwhelming urge to slap his ridiculously handsome face jolts through me as my gaze focuses on him across the room. Repressed fury continues to rise within me until my skin tickles with heat.

The memory of that one seemingly special afternoon crosses my mind occasionally but it's become almost second nature to immediately shove those thoughts away. The ink on my wrist suddenly itches, like the needle is piercing into me all over again. I suppose there will always be a reminder of my foolish heart—at least until I cover it up permanently.

I've convinced myself over the years that Rowen wasn't *the one*. But after meeting him, I became even more determined to find the *right* guy for me. Looking back on it now, there are a lot of similarities between his vanishing act and when my father abandoned me. Perhaps that's why I took Rowen's disappearance so hard back then. More recently, I've let the idea of him, and all that other fluffy love shit, lose potency. I'd been determined to move on with my life and forget about the ridiculous pipe dream I once held onto so tightly. The significance of what Rowen represented faded further with each passing season.

I'd almost tricked myself into believing he'd been a figment of my imagination, but seeing Rowen again—right in front of my effing face—I know he's freaking real. My erratic heartbeat and other uncontrollable physical reactions are evidence enough. The exponential spike in my pulse is like a high-voltage shock from the fences meant to keep horses corralled.

So yeah, there's really no denying it. Even after all this time, and the differences in his appearance, I recognize Rowen immediately.

I wonder if his sky-blue eyes shine as brightly as they did that day.

His hair is cropped short and styled in that messy way guys always pull off. A decent amount of scruff covers his jaw and it's a shade darker than the tresses on his head. His shoulders are so broad he must have trouble fitting through a regular-sized door and his biceps are so freaking huge they stretch the cotton of his shirt. I imagine the seams tearing from the strain. I guarantee he's hiding an impressive set of washboard abs behind that tight fabric because he's still clearly the standard for perfection.

My mind turns a dirty corner as I ponder what Rowen must be rocking below the belt. Considering how enormous he is *everywhere*, I bet his package is beyond impressive. And suddenly I'm freaking starving for something that isn't offered on the buffet line. Traitorous butterflies swarm my belly as heat spreads from my core and I despise the surge of pleasure this jerk elicits.

I circle back to how dumb it was to gauge Rowen as the ideal man that day. We hardly spoke a word to each other yet I placed him on a pedestal.

Our souls bonding.

His gaze reflecting the future.

My one and only.

Barf. How ridiculous.

Maybe it's not fair to place so much blame on this stranger's shoulders but I needed a scapegoat. Since he was the one that jumpstarted my belief in soul mates, he made an adequate target.

Trust me, I realize how insane I sound right now. I really do but I can't freaking help it. I know it's stupid to believe he had such an influence on me but I wanted male affection so badly that it became a driving need. I gave Rowen way too much power and it's high time I take it back.

Irritation crawls through my veins as I contemplate my choices. I'm not fucking leaving Willow and Xander's party because *he* made an appearance. I want to storm over to my friend and demand she explain why this guy was never around Xander before. Tonight is supposed to be a small gathering for close friends.

Of course Willow has zero knowledge on my history with Rowen; I've never uttered a word. I haven't shared the depth of my adversity with men and relationships. She doesn't know about my biggest downfall or slew of careless mistakes. We don't discuss my disinterest in dating. Willow's lack of awareness sends a bolt of guilt through my chest. I should have confided in her but it's not something I especially enjoy confessing.

If I attempt to gain any info on Xander's buddy now, she'll immediately dig for details. She'll most likely give me her deep stare while lifting a questioning brow and keep at it until I spill the entire story. Tonight isn't about me and the stupid decisions I've made. If I'm going to face this problem, it's up to me.

My sight locks on Rowen again as I consider my next move. He's standing across the freaking bar and he doesn't know my internal struggle. There's no way he thinks of me like I do him. Our one moment was forever ago on a typical summer day and wouldn't stand out after all this time.

Is this destiny fucking with me? Fate finally tossing me the finger for screwing around too much? A silent snicker escapes me when I think about Cupid's arrow piercing Rowen in the ass. He'd deserve to be stuck in some lover's trance but I'm done falling for any of that ludicrous shit. It's all made-up nonsense. Fairy tales and happily ever after don't exist.

With my chest clenching tight, I try imagining he's not looming before me like a long-lost dream. Who knows if it's even him? My initial reaction could be way off. Maybe Rowen has a twin who happens to know Willow and Xander. That's possible, right?

Urgh, of course it's him!

I'll never forget the delicious tingles he causes, no matter how hard I try. The stupid electricity is still zipping through me.

I glare at his perfect profile and hope the daggers I'm shooting are stabbing into his perfectly golden skin.

A devious plan takes root and the need for revenge strengthens. I spin around on my sky-high heels and strut toward the bathroom to prepare for the mission.

Once the door is locked securely behind me, I stare at my reflection in the mirror to appraise my appearance. It's time to accentuate my assets. I lift my already ample cleavage higher, making my breasts practically pop out of my top. *Perfect*. Push-up bras are freaking priceless. I coat my plump pout with bright red lipstick before fluffing my glossy platinum mane. I dyed my dull brown locks a while back when I was desperate for a change and I've never been happier with the transformation.

I look like a freaking siren and I love the thrill shooting through my entire system. It matches the burning ache I have in the pit of my stomach. He's finally going to feel my pain.

Rowen thought he could waltz into my life and hijack my fragile heart? Lie about wanting to get to know me before dashing off without a trace?

He's about to regret the day he stepped foot into Brack's Box. I'll make freaking sure he gets the fury that's been building all these years.

I stroll back into the bar with my sights set on a very particular man and one thought loops through my mind as I strut closer to him.

I'm going to make him pay.

TWO

Rowen

I f you had told me a few months ago that I'd be standing in this crowded ass bar celebrating Xander's engagement tonight, I would have laughed in your face. He was a fucking disaster when he first stumbled into our group session at the VA but I'll admit, his progress in such a short amount of time has been impressive.

I've seen plenty of guys much further along crumble under the pressure. Fighting in a war can permanently fuck up a person and many can't move on from that level of devastation. Xander came in with something to prove and pushed himself further each day. Pretty sure his fiancé has always had a lot to do with that but either way, he's a success story in the flesh. Hopefully he'll believe it someday.

Some random dude stumbles into me while trying to reach his table and it reminds me of how packed this tiny place is. Having all these bodies swarming around us makes *my* blood pressure rise so I'm not sure how Xander is managing it. Even if they're all friends and family, my skin prickles with unease. When I turn around to face my friend again, the reason he's keeping it together is blatantly obvious. I'm gifted with a front row seat to his staring contest with Willow and it's so fucking sweet my teeth ache. Even though the entire room separates them, they appear connected somehow.

I'm jealous and I don't care if that makes me sound like a jerkoff. I want that kind of all-encompassing love, and have for quite a while, but I haven't found the right woman. Well, at least not recently.

Xander's hands begin to twitch and I wonder if he's nervous or unconsciously trying to reach out for his fiancé. Seriously, they're not physically close together yet a tense tether seems bound between them. I wonder how long it will be before one of them snaps and can't handle the distance. I'm thinking the sooner, the better. They need to get a fucking room and stop rubbing it in our faces. I clear my throat to get his attention and it takes him far longer than it should to peel his eyes away from Willow. A disbelieving chuckle rattles in my chest at my friend's reluctance, but again, I'm mostly green with envy.

"I can't believe you're engaged. What a fucking trip. Has it sunk in yet?" I hope Xander isn't offended by my question. I never know with this guy. Based off the grin tipping up the corner of his lips, he isn't too upset.

"Row, I've wanted to marry that girl since I was thirteen. I'm ashamed it took me so long, and we wasted years, but whatever. She's mine now and that's what matters." His gruff voice leaves no room for argument, not like it ever would when it comes to Willow.

"Want to tell me all about when you got down on one knee?" Another laugh rolls out of me but Xander doesn't skip a beat before diving into a replay of his romantic afternoon.

He's filling me in on all the gooey details when I catch sight of a blonde bombshell sashaying our way. Her slender body is tightly wrapped in a skimpy red dress that matches the shade slathered on her lips. Voluptuous tits, made for sin, are on display for all to see and my mouth waters at the sight. All that smooth flesh is practically begging my tongue to enjoy a taste and I'm having a tough time finding reasons to resist. I tear my deprived gaze away from her cleavage before getting caught and focus on her golden mane. She has hair the color of champagne, with multiple hues blending together to make a hypnotic effect. Each strand shines and shimmer as she walks, beckoning me toward her like a moth to a flame. I want to fall into her.

Badly.

My hungry eyes wander back to her face and her shocking bronze irises appear to be glowing back at me. It's as though this lovely looker can see into my dark soul and hear my dirty thoughts—they are fucking filthy. She's put together like every man's fantasy and my dick definitely takes notice.

The last thing I need is to pitch a tent but this woman is fucking gorgeous. She deserves a standing ovation from my cock but I'm not in the mood to embarrass myself. Long legs that are perfectly toned and tan carry her our way as I attempt to discretely adjust my stubborn erection. A friendly smile stretches her mouth and my breath catches at the sight as my heart threatens to burst from overexertion. My stupid ass believes I'm the lucky recipient of her devastating grin until I realize she's focused on Xander.

Does he know this stunner?

The muttered curse from my buddy confirms they've met at least a time or two. My curiosity is instantly piqued and I'm ready to make her acquaintance. As she squeezes into the small space beside Xander and strikes up a conversation with him, I inspect her exquisite features further. She looks familiar but I can't quite place where I'd know her from. The rusty cogs in my brain groan in protest while I try recalling when we might have met. She's definitely not a woman easily forgotten.

After exchanging brief pleasantries and congratulations, the beauty shifts her sight and I'm her next target. Her vibrant orbs latch onto me and I'm hit with an overwhelming urge to haul her into my arms. To kiss her, protect her, love her.

What the fuck?

Her stare is predatory as she licks her red-stained lips. She makes my cock twitch from that move alone. She extends her tiny hand, with black painted nails, before introducing herself.

"My name is Lark. I'm good friends with Willow. And you are?" Her voice is practically a purr and recognition slams into me.

I'm transported back to when I was a completely different guy and she was definitely not a sexed up wildcat. Maybe I'm jumping the gun and shouldn't make assumptions from a name and sweet honey tone, but it's tough to ignore the coincidence when she's this close. Could this really be Lark from the restaurant? My need to know roars loudly above all else but I shove that aside as she leans closer.

Once her soft palm slides into my calloused hand and our skin touches, a certainty so sure I would bet my life on it slams into me. Shocks race up my arm to my shoulder before settling in my chest. It's like coming home, this overwhelming sense of peace that settles over me, and I can't believe it's her.

How long has it been? Six or seven years maybe? The afternoon I met her is one I'll never forget, for several reasons, and she's at the top of the list. I instantly wonder how she spends her days and who she shares her evenings with. The shock continues to radiate through my skull as the dumbfounded fog begins to clear from my brain.

Lark's fingers shift slightly in my hold, which effectively knocks me out of the stupor I'd been suspended in. She quirks an inquisitive brow my way when the silence stretches longer than socially acceptable. I realize too late that I've been standing here like an idiot, still holding her hand, without saying a word. I clear my throat to mask the lingering discomfort. "That's a beautiful name. Very fitting." I flash a flirty smile and it seems to appease her since she resumes a thorough perusal of my body.

"I'm Rowen, but all my friends call me Row. Trust me when I say it's my pleasure to meet you." It's very similar to what I said the first time I met her. I rub along the inside of her wrist in a pathetic attempt to jumpstart her memory.

Can't she feel the electricity between us?

Her heated expression hasn't changed since she spun my way so maybe she doesn't know who I am. That stings like a fucking snake bite and that ache penetrates deep when those fangs puncture skin.

Lark bites her plump bottom lip while scanning along my facial features. What does she see? Is she catching a glimpse of the younger version she might have a fuzzy recollection of? My appearance has stayed the same overall, aside from my hair that's cut shorter and darker since I don't have time to bum around the beach all day. I'm too lazy to shave so there's decent stubble covering my jaw. I've bulked up somewhat from my time in the army but I wasn't scrawny to begin with.

Acid is churning in my gut at the thought of her not remembering me. Lark should be able to recognize me if I had any impact on her. She sure acted like it that day, until I ruined it by leaving without telling her. I tried going back a few times to find her before my deployment but I never had any luck. I figured one day, if it was truly meant to be, I'd see her beautiful face again. Now she stands before me like the most delicious dessert, dressed to kill, and gladly providing fuel for my own fantasies.

Her amber eyes are like cinnamon-fire brought to life and she's scorching me on the spot.

"Aren't you a sight for sore eyes." When her words register in my distracted mind, the surprise rushes through me and my heart lodges in my throat.

"What did you say? What's that supposed to mean?" I don't

mean for my tone to come across harsh but the frustration is boiling my blood. This woman has represented something true and real in my memories for years, but the vision in front of me is fucking with my head. Desperation is clawing at my insides and I'm running out of patience.

Lark's hair glistens as she tosses her head back and laughs. "Gosh, chill out. Your face went all pale and it looks like you saw a ghost or something. I just meant you're really hot and it's been far too long since I've been graced with the presence of such a fine male specimen.

Is this chick for real? *A fine male specimen?* Who talks like that?

I refuse to believe the Lark from back then grew up to be a man eater or some shit. I've decided she's screwing with me and putting on one hell of an act.

I decide to stop messing around. "Go to dinner with me?"

"How about we go to my place instead?" Her response is instant, as though she was anticipating my request.

"Nah. Let me take you out, Sweetheart."

Lark's stunning eyes widen slightly when I let the term of endearment slip past my lips. If I hadn't been scrutinizing her so carefully, I would have missed her tiny reaction. Maybe she's affected by me after all.

Before I get another word out, she yanks her hand from my grip and twirls on her stilettos before rushing out of the bar.

That was odd as fuck. Why would she dip out so quick?

If Lark wants to pretend we haven't previously met and shared something special, I can bullshit right along with her. If she wants to storm off and hide so I have to seek her out, I'll go all in because I'm not fucking up this second chance.

Game on, Lark. Let's play.

THREE

Lark

As I stretch along my silky-soft cotton sheets, my mind plays through what I need to accomplish today. It could be a fairly easy-breezy Sunday but there is always work I can catch up on. Since I started at the community center a few years back, I've allowed my job to swallow up the majority of my free time and I prefer it that way. Idle hands and all that business.

The dull ache in the pit of my stomach reminds me of last night and my refusal to have dinner with Rowen. He could have been over here, scratching a very persistent itch, but no. He flat out denied me and I wasn't about to give into his idiotic request, so I stormed off in a furious flurry. I refuse to provide another window of opportunity to be turned down. No matter how freaking sexy he is.

An agitated scream threatens to bubble out of my mouth but I keep it in check. Ripples of shock and utter disbelief are still coiling around my brain over the fact that Rowen was at the party. Pretty sure the chances of getting struck by lightning were higher and probably less painful too. Just my stupid luck showing it's losing hand once again.

My head rolls from side to side against the fluffy pillows as my thoughts continue to race. The way Rowen looked at me made my insides hum and beg to surrender.

He's extremely dangerous to my willpower so he better keep his effing distance. That shouldn't be an issue considering he's been nothing but a hazy memory until last night. I'm not the bright-eyed, naïve girl I was seven years ago and I'll be the first to let that jackass know.

I kissed a lot of frogs during my search for "Mister Right" and with each failed attempt at finding love, my sensitive heart hardened and I became bitter. Metaphorical scars marred my body from each time I was burned by a man. Every let down felt like another lash ripping away my hope and belief in happily ever after.

Soon enough, I gave up trying and resolved myself to physical flings. I'm done with men for anything more than a quick bang to ease the occasional hunger that stirs within me. Call me whatever you want, but it's the best defense I have against further unnecessary pain. I refuse to be vulnerable again.

I'm not vindictive or diabolical but Rowen makes my blood boil. That's why I decided to give him a taste of his own medicine and formed a plan of attack. The best way to a man's heart is through his stomach or dick. I'm a terrible cook so that leaves an epic act of seduction. I'll be impossible to resist and lure him into my trap. I'm going to give Rowen the hottest, most erotic night of his life. It'll leave him fantasizing about me for years to come. And when I leave him in the dust, begging for more, I'll finally have my closure. A tad conniving, right?

Maybe there is hope for me moving past this fear of commitment once this painful chapter of my life is finally closed. I'm ready to have a healthy mindset but there have been several roadblocks forming impassible detours. The nagging insecurities have been beating down my door long enough.

That heavy dose of reality infuses me with strength and I

bounce out of bed to get ready for the day. Just as I'm walking into the bathroom, my phone pings with a message notification.

A genuine smile lifts my lips as I scan my friend's text.

> Chloe: You awake? Meet me for brunch. Pretty sure Faith will join too.

My mood brightens instantly upon receiving her invite. I'm in desperate need of some girl time to get my mind refocused. My two oldest friends don't know I ran into Rowen last night. They're going to freak the fuck out since they know all about the self-destruction I went through back then.

I can't get my response typed fast enough.

> Me: Heck yes. You are a mind reader. Where and when?

> Chloe: Sweet! Jax's Cafe in 45 minutes. See ya there.

With that settled, I continue toward the bathroom to rush through getting ready. I'm eager to get the oppressive weight of Rowen's presence off my chest.

MY TWO BESTIES are seated at a small table outside as I stroll up to the restaurant. The haste in my step makes it seem like I'm racing toward them and I'm sure the smirk on my face is ridiculous. Faith is the first to notice me.

"Oh crap, Lark has something juicy to tell us. For real. I know that look!" Her tone is light and joking as she elbows Chloe.

I'm already laughing as I take a seat across from her. They're both staring at me without saying a word. It's already clear how this chat is going to go.

I reach for their hands on the table and give them a gentle squeeze. "My ladies! I've missed you both so much. Seriously, we need to get together more often. Once or twice a month isn't cutting it." I'm aiming for nonchalance but they keep imploring me with their all-knowing glares.

"You're the one always working, Larky. I'm surprised we could pry you away today." Chloe fires back.

Faith nods while adding, "Seriously, your workaholic tendencies are getting worse. But we'll talk about that later. Give us the goods!" They lean closer, clearly prepared for dirty secrets to be revealed.

Alrighty then.

"So, guess who I ran into at Willow's engagement party?" My gaze darts between them and I attempt to wait them out. Chloe finally cracks.

"Just spit it out already. I haven't had any coffee and I don't want to spend twenty minutes playing a guessing game."

Faith giggles beside her. "Jeez, what are you cranky about? When was the last time you got laid?"

Chloe shoots her a nasty look before grumbling, "We're not talking about me right now. Spill your story, Lark."

I do exactly as she requests by saying, "Rowen."

That one word has Faith choking while Chloe looks at me with her jaw hanging open. These girls are everything I needed today. I let out a quick snort and roll my eyes before starting from the beginning.

"I'm not joking, you guys. I was minding my own business when he busted into the bar like he owned the joint. I couldn't freaking believe it! I had a mini-meltdown while trying to figure out what to do. I've imaged bumping into his sexy ass and jumping his bones before slamming into him with my truck. You know?" I can hear the tremble in my voice as I recall the shock over seeing him.

My heart starts racing and my throat tightens from the onslaught of emotions. Just talking about him gets me all worked up. For years, I wanted to provide him with an epic verbal lashing. Instead, I froze up while the residual pain washed over me and the betrayal settled deep into my gut.

Urgh, time to move on.

"I kept my distance while deciding how to approach him. Carefully formulating and scheming . . ." I continue rehashing every moment of my encounter with the guy I've never quite gotten over. Chloe and Faith are silent as they appear to be hanging on each word.

I tell them everything, starting with how devastatingly handsome Rowen looked and ending with me stomping out of the bar after he refused to fall into my trap. When I speak the final word, my shoulders seem free of the strain that had been pressing down on them. But then anxiety prickles my skin as I wait for my friends' reactions. Worry slithers down my spine that they'll tell me to steer clear. Even though that's the right response, it's not what I'm hoping for.

Chloe does exactly what a good friend should. "Obviously this jerk screwed you up, so you should stay far away. I know your bitch-ass isn't going to do that so I might as well be supportive of whatever crazy revenge plot you've cooked up." She's got laughter in her voice, which lets me know I haven't gone too far off the rails.

"You know we've got your back, Larky. I get your shock over seeing Rowen after all this time and I'm totally with you, no matter what." Faith's genuine words further strengthen my resolve to get the closure I need from this guy.

"What's your plan?" Chloe pipes in.

"Well, first I need to talk with Willow. If anyone can shed more light on this crazy situation, it should be her. I'll stop by her house after this." I respond, already switching topics in my mind. As my focus latches onto Chloe, my eyebrows lift expectantly. "Now tell me, what's got your panties in a bunch?"

She rolls her eyes dramatically while waving away my concern. "*Urgh*, just another lame date with a loser I met at the bar. Not sure why I keep trying since they're always a disappointment." Chloe blows out an exasperated sigh before pointing at me. "Larky, you're smart to have the 'screw and scram' motto. Maybe I should adopt it."

A bitter snicker bubbles up my throat. "Don't you dare. Trust me, you don't want to be a crazy spinster like me—plotting stupidly outrageous revenge on some rando who did me wrong years ago. He doesn't even remember me . . . Gosh, I have too many screws loose." Burying my face in my hands, I groan loudly before looking back at my sweet friend. "There's still hope for you, Chlo."

"Whatever, girl. You know Rowen isn't some random dude. Stop pretending." Her laugh is buoyant.

Faith agrees with a quick nod. "She's right but let's move away from this depressing shit for now. Who wants a margarita?"

Forgetting my Rowen troubles for a while sounds like the best idea yet. We spend the next few hours laughing, catching up, drinking, and definitely not obsessing about stupid guys.

FOUR

Rowen

'm spending my Sunday morning at the office and it's fucking terrible. Who wants to waste their weekend working? Nobody.

Especially when I'm horribly distracted and confused. My brain refuses to focus on the numerous tasks in front of me because all I see is Lark at the bar last night. My thoughts are preoccupied with platinum-blonde hair and what should have been. This particular woman has stolen my attention for years and apparently doesn't remember me.

I glance down at a pile of contracts in an attempt to motivate myself. My cousin, Lincoln, started Sworr Security while I was still deployed overseas. Even though I wasn't here when the doors first opened, this company is a collaboration we'd been building in our minds since middle school.

We used to hide up in his treehouse and talk for hours about this grand plan of starting a business together. Our future careers started as super-heroes to save damsels in distress but slowly shifted into protecting our community. We wanted to get rich quick and be famously successful. We believed the world was at our fingertips and all our dreams would come true. Eventually we realized it took a lot more than wild imaginations to build a business. A plan to create a security operation took place, which was actually obtainable, and we were both interested in that line of work.

A lot has happened since those initial discussions. We both enlisted in the armed forces and were deployed overseas. Through those years, we gained a lot of specialized training and skills that would be vital in our future business endeavor. Linc and I slowly realized that our pipe dream had an actual shot of becoming reality.

When I reenlisted for an additional tour, he'd already signed on the dotted line to get the fuck out. He has been for almost two years. Lincoln was ready to be his own boss and create rules. He's driven and tenacious so before I arrived back on American soil, he'd taken our scattered ideas and turned them into a little empire.

He's been busy collecting contacts and making connections, which means I'm able to sit here as the co-owner of a decent sized security company. Linc handles any contracts that require traveling out of state so I can stay local for my work at the clinic. He loves schmoozing potential clients while I prefer what happens behind the scenes. Plus, I've never been a fan of planes and got my fair share of globe-trotting during my time in the army.

I've only been discharged for six months but have managed to accomplish a lot in a short amount of time. I'm dedicated and motivated to meet any goal, which has been the case my entire life.

This is what I was meant to do and my time as a combat engineer only solidified it. I'm a lucky jackass for all the opportunities I've been given, especially in the occupational department. Since that part of my life is taken care of, I often find myself wanting more from my personal life. I'm a single man who's tired of being lonely.

Don't get me wrong. I could find plenty of female company if I was looking for a quick screw. I'm over that bullshit though.

Life is too damn short to play it so fast and loose. I'm ready for the responsibility, some actual substance, and a family of my own.

The war changed me. It changes all of us somehow. For guys like Xander, their time in the desert nearly destroys them. I consider myself somewhat fortunate that I made it out without any significant psychological damage. Well, at least none that the professionals have found.

Watching my fellow soldiers, men that became like brothers to me, die in my arms gave me some fucking perspective. Life clicked together on my last tour and I decided it was time for me to grow up. I was done wasting time on shit that didn't matter, and that included meaningless flings with forgettable faces. Prior to that, women had entered and left my life faster than I could keep track. I wasn't interested in any of them sticking around and they never made a fuss about wanting more from me either.

The war is responsible for solidifying the shift within me, but there's more to the tale. I've never considered myself romantic or sweet. Hell, not even polite most of the time. But if I'm going to be completely honest—I haven't been the same since that summer afternoon I met a very special girl.

Lark tore me apart that day—shook everything loose—and I only spent moments with her. She changed my entire outlook with just a brief touch and bashful glance. She captured my soul and my chest aches at the reminder of what I'm missing. It was as though Lark rebooted my system when she jumpstarted my heart. I never got over it.

I don't need grand gestures or public displays of affection to understand someone cares. I know what devotion and adoration look like—all I have to do is hang out with Xander and Willow to get a large dose of it. I also grew up with parents that were crazy about one another, even after decades of marriage.

And I know what true love feels like as everything inside of me suddenly clicks into place. When my skin sets on fire in desperation to connect with another person's body. There's an indescribable pull as my soul is claimed and no longer belongs to me.

I had that type of connection and lost it as Lark slipped through my fingers, never to be seen or heard from again. Everything could be different if my phone had stayed silent and all hell hadn't broken lose at base during those same unforgettable moments. Our whispered words from that day rush to the forefront of my mind. We belong together and I'm determined to prove how much she means to me.

When did I become such a fucking sap?

I find myself obsessing over her yet barely know who she is. Lark makes me want to get down on my knees and beg for her attention, which scares the fuck out of me. At the same time, it seems so right that my entire being sighs with relief at the idea of giving into her. I won't though—not until she understands where I'm coming from and what I truly desire.

It's been over three years since I've had sex or even felt a woman's touch. Some nights are damn difficult but I have enough self-control to keep my head in the game. My hand does the trick but it's lost appeal lately. I haven't been tempted until a certain stunner strutted into my view. Some sort of higher power must be shining down on me now because I've been given another shot, and this time I won't fuck it up.

No matter how hot Lark is, I'm not throwing away my strict principles for one night of filthy fun. When I put an end to my celibacy, it will be for the real deal. I've always appreciated a challenge and there is a noticeable tightening in my groin when I think of her making me work for what I want. I'm going to reach this goal too. She just doesn't know it yet.

I'm certain Lark is the one I've been waiting for but our interaction last night left me with a heap of questions. Her frosty attitude gave me a chill that's still pinching my skin. She's clearly not the woman I remember and my heart plummets when I consider the reasons why. Lark is no longer the shy girl that blushed when I flirted with her. Now she's a predatory vixen ready to sink her claws into the next victim. I'm a man with a new mission—and I won't shy away—so she better be ready.

It's become glaringly obvious that I'm not getting any work done now that I let my thoughts wander. I push away from the desk to clutch my pounding head with my clammy hands. Lark already has me twisted up in so many knots I can't keep anything straight.

I had planned to discuss the woman of my dreams with Xander after she scampered off, but he got whisked away by Willow before I had the chance. I should swing by his place and beg for some scraps of intel. I know Lark works with Willow so they've got to have some insight on who she is these days. Hopefully I can get them on my side and rooting for my love-struck ass.

Then I'll work on getting my future on board with this plan.

FIVE

Lark

Thank goodness for great friends, right?

Spending time with Faith and Chloe lifted my spirits exponentially and my mood has been totally rejuvenated. Positivity thrums through me as I glide along the sidewalk toward Willow's house.

The quaint yellow rambler could be featured in a Norman Rockwell painting, especially with the happy couple living inside. Their beautiful home is nestled on an expansive lawn that I'm constantly jealous of. It's rare to find an entire acre of land this close to downtown but Willow managed to snag this place without paying a fortune.

I bounce up her steps and ring the bell. The door swings open almost immediately—as though Willow was standing directly on the other side waiting. When she turns to face me, her eyes widen noticeably as she jerks back a step. The shock is obvious on her face and my own features tighten in confusion from her reaction.

She peeks her head outside in order to glance both ways down the street, and that makes me even more curious. When Willow straightens back up, she looks at me with the same wary expression. She continues staring at me without uttering a word. It's becoming awkward.

I wave my hand in front of her face while saying, "What's your deal?"

She seems to snap out of her surprise with a slight shake of her head. "Hey Lark. Sorry, I just wasn't expecting you and it's slightly weird timing. Do you want to come in?"

"What do you mean by 'weird timing'?" I make those stupid air quotes with my fingers because she's not making any sense.

"Nothing. Forget about it. Are you here to hang out or what?" She's got a bit of sass in her tone as she waves me inside.

Willow steps out of the way before closing the door behind me. She begins wandering into the dining room where Xander is sitting so I grab her hand and drag her down the hallway. My sights are set on the bathroom for some privacy.

She stumbles from my hasty move but this whole situation has put me back on edge. The irritation from Rowen's unexpected appearance bubbles back to the surface. There is a lot I need to get off my chest and I've always favored ripping the bandage off. I click the lock after getting us inside, prepared to get some freaking answers.

Before a word can be spoken, the door flies open and bangs against the wall. The wood edge barely misses my shoulder. My heart leaps into my throat as my pulse takes off at a sprint. What the actual eff is going on here today?

Xander is looming in the threshold—looking absolutely terrifying—wildly scanning the room as his chest heaves with uneven breaths. His enormous fists shake at his sides while his frantic gaze seeks out Willow behind me. My head swivels back and forth between them for a moment while I attempt to regain my freaking bearings.

"X, are you alright?" Willow's voice is full of concern as she squeezes past me. Her palm reaches up to cup his cheek while confusion once again plows into me.

"Are you kidding me right now? You're apart all the time!" My words come out squeaky with alarm. I realize my mistake about two seconds too late.

"Hey!" Willow's tone is sharp and cracks through the small space we're huddled in. "Don't you dare start with that judgmental crap. We have an open door policy in this house. You're the one who barged in unannounced."

Willow is usually pretty breezy unless her fiancé is involved. Right now, she's practically foaming at the mouth and ready to bite my head off for potentially offending him. Guilt flashes up my spine because they don't deserve my snarky attitude. She glares at me for another moment before swinging her gaze to Xander and the frustration instantly melts off her form.

The smile stretching Willow's lips is reserved just for him and it cools the tension that's been simmering in my veins since this morning. I release a content sigh and relax my body against the wall. This level of love and happiness is the ultimate dream, right? At least for some people. I'll never find it but at least they have it. I suppose this is proof soul mates actually exist in very rare instances.

"I'm really sorry that I stormed in here and caused an issue. Why don't I just leave and we can talk tomorrow." I utter the apology softly so I don't disrupt their peaceful bliss. My eyes are locked on Willow and I hope she forgives me for being a brat. When she looks my way—her eyes clear of strain and anger—the weight on my chest disappears.

Willow sends me a haughty smirk before saying, "One day you'll figure it out."

That comment causes me to roll my eyes because she is always trying to show me the light. Once we chat about Rowen, maybe she'll finally understand my resistance. I push off the wall and get ready to see myself out when Xander speaks.

"Stay, Lark. I'll give you two some space but don't shut me out." He's gruff and growly but I see distinct tenderness as he keeps his eyes locked on Willow. She tilts her chin up and their lips meet, which causes Xander to groan as he yanks her closer. Combustible heat fills the bathroom and awkwardness slams down on me while I get another intense display of their chemistry. I'm obviously in their way and should get the eff out of here.

Just as I'm about to clear my throat and excuse myself, Willow breaks away from Xander and stumbles back into me. She giggles like a schoolgirl and I can't hold back the scoff that escapes me. I can handle a lot but now they're just rubbing it in.

Willow glances at me over her shoulder before wiggling her eyebrows suggestively. She is so ridiculous and I can't help laughing at her little stunt. Xander hums, effectively gaining both our attention, while devouring Willow with his hungry stare. He bites his lip while backing away and the temperature instantly decreases once he's out of view.

Good God, that was like watching a freaking porno intro.

Oblivious to my thoughts, Willow whips around to face me and a dopey smile lights up her entire face.

"So chica, what's up with you?"

Now she's ready to talk. Super.

"I actually wanted to talk about a guy from the party last night. I think he's one of Xander's friends but I hadn't met him before. I believe his name is Rowen." I send a skeptical brow her way as recognition seems to plow into her.

Thankfully I don't have to bother digging for clues since Willow gives it all away the instant his name leaves my lips. She might as well have a huge neon sign above her head considering how obvious it is that she knows him. Her breath hitches as she sucks in air through her clenched teeth and her eyes get squinty like she's in pain—or is hiding some juicy information.

I roll my eyes—so hard they hurt—while scoffing again so she knows I'm privy to her blatant visual cues. I purse my lips and proceed to wait her out.

Willow crosses her arms across her chest before uttering, "What?"

"You can't play coy. Why hasn't Rowen come around before? Tell me what you know about him."

"I hardly *know* him." She puts far too much emphasis on that one word. "We've met a handful of times at the clinic since Rowen leads one of the groups Xander is in. There have been a few other random occurrences but never anything planned really. Xander isn't a huge fan of people in general. Why are you so interested in him?" Willow points an accusatory finger at me before scoffing herself. "Do you like this guy?"

I ignore her question entirely. "When were these unplanned situations? How is it I just met him last night if Xander has known him for a while?"

It's her turn to ignore what I've asked. "What's your deal, Lark? You're acting super suspicious."

"I don't have a deal. Did you see the guy? He's super-hot and you've clearly been holding out on me."

Willow is already shaking her head dramatically before I finish talking.

"Oh, no. Nope. Not happening, Lark. I love you like a work-wife but Rowen is not the type of guy for you."

"What the fuck, Willow! What's that supposed to mean?" I can hear the offended hurt in my voice.

"Rowen is not the screw around type—that's all. If you're finally looking for a relationship, that's great, but I won't encourage this so you can just use him for sex. He wants more than that." She places a hand on my arm in an attempt to comfort me but I immediately pull away from her hold.

"How do you know that? I thought Rowen doesn't really hang out with Xander? You seem to know plenty of his personal preferences." I can hear the accusations dripping from my tone and I need to harness my crap before this turns into a serious argument.

I rub my face while a frustrated sigh swooshes past my lips. "I'm sorry, Willow. I don't have the right to get so freaking worked up, especially when you don't know why." I glance at her from the corner of my eye while contemplating how much of the truth to reveal.

Willow raises a curious brow my way. "What's really going on here Lark? There's more to the story."

A loud huff escapes my throat while I dramatically wave my hand around to signal she's talking nonsense. I don't think I'm ready to admit my crazy to her just yet.

She tries a different approach and I see her technique from a mile away. "You know my fiancé right? He's super private and hardly leaves the house except for therapy and when absolutely necessary. I mean, just recently he started going to visit his parents and taking on a few odd jobs. It's not like he's been hanging out with Rowen at the bar every night. I haven't been hiding some bromance relationship but you are most definitely keeping something from me."

I release a defeated puff of air and decide to fill her in—at least a little bit. She's clearly not going to be on Team Revenge so I'll be keeping my plan of attack locked away.

"All right, all right. I've actually met Rowen before but that was years ago when I was still a stupid girl desperate for love. He came into the restaurant where I worked and we shared a moment. Nothing extraordinary or meaningful, as it turned out." The resentment bleeds from my words but Willow doesn't comment so I keep going.

"I've told you about my dad leaving and the train wreck that is my dating history. Well, Rowen is a tiny part of that puzzle and fairly insignificant." I raise my thumb and forefinger to show just how small I'm trying to make him seem. "He doesn't even remember me based off our awkward conversation yesterday so forget him." The need to downplay Rowen's impact on me seems like a protective shield that guards my heart—even from one of my closest friends.

I'm such a fraud.

Before I can vomit more useless information, Willow responds with, "Interesting." That's all she says while I'm wound so freaking tight my muscles ache.

"What is?" I snap while desperately wanting to flick her in the forehead for being such an unhelpful brat.

She smirks before her finger circles in front of my face. "You're crazy about this guy."

"That's completely ludicrous." I retort without pause.

Of course Willow sees right through me and goes for the jugular. "Uh huh. Sure. So, I suppose it isn't a huge deal that he happened to be here right before you showed up."

What the actual eff-bomb?! It's like the rug is pulled out from under me and the move knocks me off my feet. I think the ground might actually be tilting.

Instead of screaming at the top of my lungs like I really want to do right about now, I try to remain calm and reply with total nonchalance.

"Well that's a weird coincidence. Is that why you were acting so strange when I first got here?

"I was acting strange? Lark, you're smoking oats if you believe this entire conversation is anything close to normal. I don't know why you are so concerned with Rowen but maybe I should ask him." The sass is back in her voice as she serves that volley. Willow is a worthy opponent, which is probably why we're good friends.

Freaking figures she wouldn't give me any decent information without knowing exactly why I want it. Willow isn't aware that I'm preparing for battle against this man and she's going to help me win.

SIX

Rowen

The utter emptiness of my house is suffocating—which doesn't make a ton of sense—and I can't seem to inhale a decent breath. The silence surrounds me and my only companion is the relentless pounding in my skull. I sag further back on the couch and try to settle my erratic thoughts. It's no use.

All I see is bright blonde hair and ruby red lips.

Ever since I spoke to Willow a few days ago, I've been obsessing over each word she shared regarding Lark. She was very willing to give information, especially once my intentions were clear. Willow is the most hopeless romantic I've ever met so the idea of me pursuing Lark made her giddy.

That doesn't help my current situation—especially since the woman I'm fantasizing about sharing a life with only wants me for sex. Willow confirmed Lark's serial screwing habits and informed me that she's never witnessed her friend go out with the same man twice. Though she was quick to assure me even *that* is rare, since Lark is always at work. That is depressing as hell and again has me wondering why she refuses to consider anything more than a quick fuck.

Willow believes Lark is waiting for the right guy to stumble along but based on her relatively indifferent reaction to me on Saturday, the one she's searching for isn't me. That doesn't mean I'm going to give up. Especially since the outrageous chemistry we once shared still burns in the back of my mind. That was ages ago but where there's a will, there's a way.

An agonized groan rumbles through my chest as I continue picturing the sexy vixen I met in the bar. She's drop-dead gorgeous and ready to sink her teeth into a juicy piece of meat. That woman was wearing a mask so thick, it wasn't possible to see underneath it. I imagine Lark's blinding beauty as she looked that night but my vision injects her soft demeanor from the past. The combination is what my dreams are made of—ultimate perfection.

Don't get me wrong, I was insanely attracted to Lark when I first met her. That's why I couldn't stop obsessing over the possibility of seeing her again. Seven years ago, we were teenagers so it's creepy to keep that version playing in my fantasy reel, especially when I have the adult model fresh in my arsenal.

Thanks to Willow, I have Lark's phone number but I've been too chicken shit to use it. Tonight the heartache is flowing freely through my veins—thanks to the extra dose of pathetic this isolated house makes me feel—so I decide to send her a message. I have absolute temptation at my fingertips so why the hell not.

I deliberate for a few moments over what to type then decide to keep it simple.

> Me: Hey Lark. This is Rowen, Xander's friend from the bar on Saturday. Willow gave me your number. How's it going?

Since the little vixen didn't appear to remember meeting me before, I'll play along and keep up the ruse. Soon enough, I'll bring that summer afternoon back to the surface.

I stare at my phone far too long, secretly wishing for a reply. After five minutes of radio silence, I consider heading to the gym to burn off some excess energy. It's either that or watch porn, which doesn't appeal to me unless Lark is the star.

Just as I'm stretching my stiff muscles from hours of lounging, a notification alert echoes throughout the quiet room. The leap my heart takes is fucking embarrassing but the fact she responded gives me hope. That is until I read her message.

> Lark: *There were a lot of Xander's friends I met that night. Which one were you?*

Irritation boils my blood that we're pretending not to know each other. I hate playing this stupid game but if this keeps her responding, I'll go along with it for now.

> Me: *Popular lady. I'm not surprised. We met at the end of the evening. You left after I offered to take you out for dinner.*

This time her reply is immediate.

> Lark: *Fine Male Specimen?*

This woman will surely be the death of me.

> Me: *I prefer Rowen, or Row. Let me take you out tonight.*

I purposely make that a statement, not a request. She isn't falling for it though.

> Lark: *Perhaps I wasn't clear on Saturday. I'm not interested in dating. If you're in the mood for something spicy though . . .*

> Me: *What's with the sex obsession? Are you seeing a professional for your addiction?*

Once the words are sent, regret sinks deep into my gut. We're not nearly close enough to joke around about that shit—especially over text message. Her response is exactly what I expect.

Lark: Fuck off.

I'm a fucking disaster where she's concerned but I'm not ready to back down.

> *Me: That was a shitty thing to say and I'm sorry. I just want the chance to know you and I'm screwing it up. Can we start over?*

I don't expect a response so when the three little dots suddenly appear, I'm certain my eyes are messing with me.

> *Lark: There is no reason to start over when nothing ever began. I'm sure you're a great guy but I'm not interested.*

I gawk at my phone as shock filters into my tired brain. Are these mind games or is she really trying to shake me loose? Wasn't she just trying to lure me between her sheets?

Discouragement lands heavy on my chest like a lead weight and I'm at a total loss for what to do next. It's like being kicked when I'm already down. Except Lark isn't aware of my infatuation with her. At least that's what she's leading me to believe.

While I'm participating in a pity-party for one, my phone pings with another message—and I'm almost afraid to read it.

> *Lark: Unless you're willing to skip dinner and go straight for dessert . . .*

I shake my head as a humorless chuckle wheezes from my parched throat. She came back for more after I didn't feed into her little power play. A surge of adrenaline courses through my weary bones as I contemplate my next move. Lark can try pushing me away but I'm not going anywhere without a damn good fight.

It's been less than a week and I'm ready to lock this situation down so the girl I've been fantasizing over is officially mine. I want it all with her and it seems like the best type of luck that we met again. She might not be in the same mindset as me, at least not yet, but I'll work hard to earn her trust back. Maybe that's what second chances are for.

I'm going to make it impossible for Lark to deny me—starting now.

$$\ggg\!\!\!-\!\!-\!\!\heartsuit\!\!-\!\!-\!\!\to$$

SHE TURNED OUT to be extremely resistant to my advances via text so I didn't make much progress last night. Instead of continuing to argue with Lark, I let her know she'd see me soon but I don't think she took me seriously. I'm in this for the long haul.

Pretty sure I'm the farthest thing from a candy-and-hearts type of guy but for this girl, I find myself wanting to do whatever it takes. Starting with the extravagant bouquet of Calla lilies I'm currently carrying into her office. Thanks to Willow, I know these are Lark's favorite flowers and apparently no one has taken the time to deliver them to her before.

I'm hoping this gesture places me a little closer to Lark's good side but this little vixen likes to keep me guessing. Though it's past six o'clock in the evening, I've been assured she's still at the community center, working hard for the troubled youth she counsels. If I wasn't already sure this girl was the one for me, her chosen profession would definitely seal the deal. Lark is clearly a giver with an empathetic soul and that further proves how special she is.

Once I'm standing outside her door, I pause to take a calming breath as I prepare what to say. I shouldn't have bothered because as I step into her office, my brain short-circuits at the glorious sight before me. My cock takes notice too as my pants become unmistakably tighter. A little discomfort is fucking worth this.

Lark is seated behind her cluttered desk and staring at her computer screen, which emphasizes her flawless features with a luminous glow. She hasn't seen me yet so I'm able to silently appreciate her a bit longer. I'm ogling like a fucking creeper but she's too irresistible. It's like choosing to drop into enemy territory, and even though you probably won't make it out alive, you could potentially save a thousand. This is absolutely worth the risk.

Today she looks much closer to the Lark I remember from all those years ago. She's dressed in a simple blue shirt that reaches her collarbone. Her long blonde locks are tied up in a messy bun. Lark's lips are a natural shade of pink and I'm immediately imagining how soft they'll be when my tongue traces her delectable pout. A pair of black-rimmed glasses are perched on her button nose, which completes the extremely sexy look she's owning. I have to bite back a groan because I'm sure Lark won't be pleased to discover me lurking—especially if I'm salivating all over her.

Before my dick takes complete control of my thoughts, I clear my throat slightly to make my presence known but keep the flowers hidden for now. Lark's gaze swings toward me and her brown eyes widen noticeably behind the lenses. She swivels around before standing up and leaning forward with her palms flat on the desk.

Lark shoots me a glare before asking, "What are you doing here?"

The venom in her voice is probably meant to scare me away but all I hear is *come closer*. I'm totally mesmerized.

"Hey, Sweetheart. I said you'd be seeing me soon. Figured I'd stop by and say hello in person." I make sure to keep my tone calm but my skin itches with heat at the fire burning from her gaze.

"And I told you to leave me alone unless you're ready to give me what I want." She shifts her stare down to my groin while raising an expectant brow. "Is that what you've brought me?" She lifts her scorching eyes back to my face and seductively bites into her bottom lip.

Her sass is tantalizing but it's the beauty underneath I'm truly after. "Sorry to disappoint you but that's not why I'm here, Vix. I want to discuss some stuff, relating to us."

"Vix? As in the vapor rub?"

An amused chuckle bounces up my throat. "Nah, short for Vixen."

She seems to mull it over with a slight tilt of her head. "I suppose that's fitting, though you don't need to be handing out nicknames. Tell me, what could we possibly have to talk about?"

"No idle chit-chat first? I'm hoping we can get to know each other. I haven't been able to stop thinking about you since the other night and this sexy librarian look you're rocking is hot as hell, but it's more than that. Are you willing to hear me out? Maybe make an exception for me?"

A frustrated sigh answers my question. "I don't have the patience for this, Rowen. I'm very busy here and you're wasting my time."

I lean against the door, trying to show I'm not ready to leave quite yet. "Answer me this. Where did you work when you were younger? Let's say seven years ago?"

Lark glances away before shuffling some papers into piles. Her fidgeting makes me smile because now I'm certain she remembers just fine. A barely-there blush blooms on her cheeks while she continues avoiding my question. I wait her out and soon enough she graces me with a response.

"I don't see how that's any of your business." Her deflection causes me to edge forward a bit, as though we need to be closer. She speaks to the depths of my soul, no matter if she gives me sass or softness.

"I'm trying here, Vix. Want to help me out? Did you work at Brack's Box during the summer of 2010? Maybe a guy stopped in on a random July afternoon and stumbled over his words in your stunning presence. Do you remember that?"

Lark is still avoiding eye contact but I hear her whispered *yes* as if she shouted it across the room.

With her head tipped down, it's impossible to determine

her reaction but my heart is practically beating out of my chest. The need to be near her continuing to push me further into her space as I take several more steps into the office before making my confession.

"I've thought of you every day since we first met, Sweetheart. I knew you looked familiar at the bar but wasn't sure until—"

"Stop talking." Lark cuts me off easily as she raises her chin to face me. If looks could kill, I'd be six feet under. "You knew who I was but didn't say anything? You must enjoy making me feel like an idiot." She spits the words out through clenched teeth.

"Vix—"

"That's not my fucking name." Her voice is practically a growl.

I raise my hands up in an apologetic manner before responding. "I'm sorry, Lark. It's never been my intention to make you feel like an idiot. I truly want the chance to explain." I release a deep exhale. "Apparently you knew who I was and didn't mention it either. Am I right?"

"I'm not the one who fucking left!" She practically screams at me and her voice is full of agony. The sharp sound pierces my ears, and I wince. I'm floundering for what to say as my mouth opens and closes several times, like a gaping fish.

My hands tremble and remind me of the surprise still hidden. I slowly reveal the flowers and hope she won't throw them at my head, but I'd deserve it. When she catches sight of the bouquet, a quiet gasp escapes her quivering lips as her eyes fill with tears. Guilt swarms my system like toxic poison and it feels like I've been punched in the stomach.

I shouldn't have pushed so fast.

I should have tried harder to find her again.

I should have immediately confessed to remembering her that night.

I hold the lilies out and Lark blindly grabs at them without really looking. She turns away while wiping at her cheeks, which makes the pit in my stomach grow deeper.

Lark murmurs, "I think it's best if you go now." Her dejected tone stabs painfully at my soul.

"Can we please talk, Lark?" The plea easily falls from my lips because I don't want to leave. Not ever again.

Her shoulders hunch and shake slightly as she stays turned away. "I'm not interested, Rowen."

My feet carry me closer as though pulled by an invisible rope. The need to comfort her rages within me. "Please, Sweetheart. I didn't mean to upset you and I'm so fucking sorry I didn't tell you who I was right away. *Please*." Begging doesn't bother me, not with her. Lark is too fucking important to lose.

"Not now. Maybe some other time," she mutters almost silently.

Obviously I've done some serious damage to our already turbulent non-relationship. The threat of her never forgiving me feels like a blade stabbing into my heart. Overwhelming sadness crashes over me as I remain frozen in place, unsure what the right choice is. My fingers itch with the desire to touch her but I hold back.

"Can you look at me, Lark? I'll go but I want to apologize first." My tone bleeds with sorrow at her resistance.

Her head is already shaking before I finish talking and she doesn't utter another word. If there is any chance for us, I better do as she says and get gone. Even though that's the last thing I want, it's clear she's not comfortable with me here. With a parting glance her way, I turn toward the door.

I refuse to take off without a bit of hope for the future so I murmur to her quietly over my shoulder. "For what it's worth, I'm really sorry for any pain I've caused you. I hope you believe me. I'll leave for now but this isn't the end, Lark."

As I step out of her office, I'm certain she whispers, "It's only the beginning."

SEVEN

Lark

F riday mornings at the teen counseling center are fairly quiet, especially during the summer months. All the kids would rather sleep late than attend a therapy group. I don't necessarily blame them—they should enjoy it while they can. I don't remember the last time I spent a few extra hours laying around in bed.

Adulting sucks.

I'm using the downtime to catch up on paperwork and reports, but I find myself pretty preoccupied with a particular situation and a certain guy. I've been distracted by Rowen and his flower delivery since he stepped foot into my office last week. Thinking about him gets me so frustrated that I almost start banging my head against the desk.

When Rowen randomly dropped by here, I was completely unprepared. Work is my safe haven and he trampled all over it. I wasn't dressed for seduction and the polished mask to hide my insecurities wasn't in place. What Rowen saw was the real me and I wasn't effing ready for that.

When he asked about my job growing up, I *knew* he

remembered me. Pain blasted through me like an avalanche and I didn't know what to do. I was immediately transported back to the fateful day when shit started hitting the fan. Hate for Rowen boiled like acid in my veins but love burned brighter. I couldn't escape the useless emotion, even though I've attempted to forget more times than I can count. I tried to be indifferent and unaffected but I am so fucking ruined. There's no faking it.

Something in him speaks to me in a way I can't hide from. My soul perks up and demands I listen whenever he's involved. I tried to wear the bitter bitch shield but it was an epic failure. He plowed through it like a flimsy piece of tinfoil.

I can't handle Rowen sweet and romantic. I was having a difficult enough time rejecting his advances before he released the charm. He might as well have been reciting poetry for how hard I was swooning. He brought me flowers, which no man has done before.

The blooming bouquet of Calla lilies are not only my favorite blossoms but the bouquet is absolutely stunning. Willow is such a freaking traitor for selling my secrets to the enemy. She tried denying any involvement but her Cheshire grin was a dead giveaway. She kept up the innocent act by asking who they were from, as if she didn't know.

How do I even stand a chance when my own friends are double-crossing me and taking Rowen's side?

The impressive arrangement is still begrudgingly displayed on my desk and one glance brings tears to my eyes all over again. There was no way I could toss them in the trash, even if the sight of them whispers about giving him a chance. I need to get my shit together but it's a serious challenge when reminders keep blasting into my brain—like Rowen's little nicknames for me. Sweetheart was bad enough but then he took it a step further. Of course that sent my already frantic heart into another traitorous tailspin.

Stupid, stupid, stupid.

Where was this guy when I needed him? Now I'm past the point of no return and there is no going back. Pretty sure Rowen has lost interest anyway.

Since he walked out my door, I haven't heard a peep. I'm trying to convince myself to be happy about the reprieve but it clearly isn't working out so well.

I need my reliable anger to remain locked in place if I'm going to survive this unpredictable onslaught from him. Rowen needs to pay for the pain he caused me and I refuse to roll over and beg for another serving of suffering. I can't let fluffy emotions get involved and ruin my revenge.

He can't change my mind with a few sweet words and kind gestures. I don't need assistance falling for him. My armor is back in place and I won't let him crack it again.

What I really need is a different type of distraction, which gives me an idea. Friday nights are meant for going out and letting loose, so that's exactly what I'll do.

With visions of a relaxing evening as motivation, I shove the other nonsense away and focus on my piles of work. Soon enough, I'm lost in case notes and session planning before the kids arrive for group.

The familiar tasks keep my mind occupied and I manage to accomplish far more than usual by four o'clock in the afternoon. This independent, career driven woman has regained control and beams with productivity pride. I give myself a mental high-five and decide to leave a bit early as a reward.

Take that, Rowen.

MINNEAPOLIS HAS AN active nightlife with plenty of options. I chose this bar because it's right around the corner from my apartment and they offer a tasty selection of mixed drinks, which I gladly overindulge in.

The appealing scenery definitely doesn't hurt either. There are several attractive men dispersed around the space and I'm perusing the crowd between sips of my cocktail. Not that I'm interested in any of that tonight, but there's no harm in looking.

This particular watering hole is an extremely popular place for after work de-escalation since it's near an ever crowded bus stop. It's always packed so I was pleased to find several open seats when I first arrived. Maybe Chloe and Faith want to join me. They'll definitely appreciate this meat market.

As I'm polishing off my first Moscow Mule, a handsome guy approaches and sits on the stool next to me. I don't acknowledge him because I'm not in the mood for company. My lack of attention doesn't dissuade him though.

He clears his throat loudly before leaning into my personal space. "Hey, gorgeous. What are you doing here all alone?"

Urgh.

It's already painfully obvious he's over here to hit on me. Usually I'd be flattered, but today his chances are definitely zero. I don't want to encourage him but it's hard to be rude unless he deserves it.

"Enjoying a drink after a stressful week. You?"

"The same." He sticks his hand out while saying, "I'm Ronald. And you are?"

When his name registers, I internally cringe but make sure to keep the plastic smile plastered on my face. My palm slides into his for the customary shake and no sparks or tingles erupt from the connection—not that I was expecting anything extraordinary from this stranger.

"I'm Lark. It's nice to meet you." I say while scanning his features.

Ronald is very handsome with thick chestnut hair and expressive toffee eyes but no desire sparkles within me.

I remove my hand from his grip so I can flag down the

bartender for another cocktail. As I'm raising my chin to signal him, Ronald skims his fingers down my arm. This time the grin does slip from my lips.

I stare down at the offending touch before slowly shifting my glare to the guy who thought that was a smart move. He doesn't get the message from my look alone so I angle back, out of his reach. Screw being polite if this guy wants to invade my space.

Just as I'm about to tell him off, my phone lights up with a text notification. I snatch it up as an easy excuse and hopefully an obvious hint for Mr. Handsy to take a hike. I was pleased about the convenient distraction until the sender's name comes into view.

Rowen: What do you think you're doing?

Taking a chance with Ronny is my preferred choice at the moment, even if it's to tell him I'm not interested.

Then a familiar voice whispers into my left ear—immediately causing shivers to flare up everywhere as heated jitters burst between my legs. "Ignoring my messages? That's not very nice, Vix."

A strong woodsy-cedar scent floats into the air surrounding me and as I twist slightly to catch a glimpse of the intruder over my shoulder. Rowen sounds calm but one glance at his clamped jaw and flaring nostrils leads me to believe he isn't relaxed at all. Surprise causes my heart to skip beats as I contemplate the possibility of him stumbling upon me by accident. I went seven years without so much as a glimpse of him. Now he's suddenly popping up everywhere. What the hell is up with that?

My snarky mask easily slips into place. "Stalking me now? Isn't that sweet. Barging into my workspace clearly wasn't enough. You're invading my personal downtime as well." Thorns of frustration poke at me before I inhale a deep breath and turn toward my newly acquired safeguard. "Look who's here, Ronny! This is Casper, a friend-of-a-friend of sorts." I wrinkle my nose while shooting him a disapproving scowl.

"Who the hell are you referring to with a name like that?" Rowen practically spits through clenched teeth and I wonder what's got him so upset—the nickname or the other man vying for my attention?

I point at him and respond, "You, duh. You're like a fucking ghost. Disappearing in the blink of an eye like that." I snap my fingers for shock value. "It's extremely appropriate. What do you think, Ronny?" My gaze swings back to my new pal and the guy just stares at me questioningly, probably wondering if I'm worth the effort.

My attention is drawn back to Rowen as he growls, "What are you doing, Lark?"

"What the hell does it look like? I'm spending some quality time with my friend so why don't you mind your own business," I fire back while raising a haughty brow.

Ronny decides to pipe up from the sidelines. "I actually prefer Ronald, not Ronny."

Urgh.

Why couldn't he just keep his mouth shut? Now I look like a bigger fool. And *Ronald*? Barf. His name is such a turnoff. He would have been much hotter as John or Ben.

"Why are you doing this, Lark? You don't even know this guy." Rowen speaks to me as though Ronald hadn't said a word, as he hooks his thumb in the other man's direction.

"You offering me something better?"

"Yeah. Have a drink with me."

I scoff and roll my eyes. "I want a lot more than that."

I'm ogling Rowen's body in an overt manner when Ronny—I refuse to call him Ronald in my head—barges into our conversation again.

How rude is he?

"Lark and I were getting to know each other." His serious stare is locked on Rowen. "Maybe you should find another girl, buddy. She's mine tonight."

Seriously?

This guy is making my lady parts shrivel up. No way is this happening, not even a tiny bit. I almost gag. How did I think he was attractive a few minutes ago?

These two idiots continue their pissing match while effectively ignoring me. I huff out a few frustrated breaths since my plan for a drama-free night has been spoiled.

I decide to remove myself from this outrageous situation completely. The point of going out tonight was to relax and this place lost the appeal once Ronny sat down next to me. Since Rowen's focus is elsewhere, he doesn't notice me slip off the bar stool and saunter to the bathroom in my sky-high heels. A few guys attempt to catch my gaze but I am so over it.

All I want is an extra-large glass of wine while I soak in my claw-foot tub, letting the stress that's been weighing me down slowly melt away. I'm envisioning the lavender-scented bubbles and soothing music filling my ears when someone grabs my arm and spins me around.

I stumble in my Kate Spade stilettos but Rowen's grip keeps me upright. Once I find my balance, I lock my furious glare on him and prepare to ream his ass out. The words stick in my throat like super glue when I catch sight of Rowen's flushed face and stony expression. His body seems to vibrate with anger so I try stepping back, but his hold is iron-clad.

Rowen's penetrating gaze sears into me, like he's trying to read my thoughts. The level of intensity sends jolts of nervousness buzzing along my flesh but I can't look away. He has me completely transfixed, waiting for the verbal lashing I'm sure to receive.

When Rowen finally speaks after staring into my eyes for countless moments his voice is shockingly gentle.

"It's time you and me had a talk."

EIGHT

Rowen

When I'd first stepped into Drake's and spotted Lark, I couldn't believe my luck. I zeroed in on her like a sniper's target, placed in my direct line of sight and ready to make my dreams come true. She was wearing another skin-tight dress that accentuated her assets, including very toned thighs that were crossed and pointing toward a neighboring stool.

That's when I noticed the asshole seated next to her, stroking a finger down her silky arm. Murderous red consumed my vision and I began seething on the spot. I'm not an overly aggressive man but at that moment, I was prepared to rip that fucker's head off for touching her. I tried taking several calming breaths but air just hissed through my tight jaw.

Since we didn't leave off on the best terms last week, I wasn't going to plow into her space and mark my territory, even though that's exactly what my instincts demanded. Livid rage simmered within my muscles as they continued chatting so I took a timeout by texting her. My hands were shaking as I typed on the screen but my words sent. When I saw her glance at the phone and proceed to ignore my message, I'd had all I could take.

Now Lark is standing before me, in the dimly lit hallway, with wariness marring her beautiful features. I can see questions swirling in the depths of her caramel eyes as she attempts to move away from me. The last thing I want is for her to be fearful of me but I had to stop her from fleeing. This woman causes possessiveness like I've never felt before, to thunder through me. I'm controlled by the overwhelming need to make her understand how deeply I care for her. I want her to be my everything, yet she's spending time with random posers like *Ronald*. We need to clear the air and set shit straight.

My fingers are still wrapped around Lark's bicep and the connection to her is keeping my temper under control. When her soft skin met my rough palm, serenity replaced madness and the tension that was strangling me finally eased.

"It's time you and me had a talk."

Lark nods silently while keeping her gaze locked on me. I lead her further down the narrow corridor until I find the door for a storage room.

She doesn't resist as we enter the dark space and helps me search for the light. I find the dangling string and yank until the fluorescent bulb burns bright. I turn to face her and know this won't be an easy win for me. Lark crosses her arms while popping her hip out before a confident smirk lifts her ruby lips. This girl is ready for battle so I need to get my point across.

"Were you really interested in that guy out there? *Fuck*, Vix. Seeing you with him just about pushed me over the edge." I take a deep breath and try relaxing the strain in my shoulders. "Sweetheart, I know you're pissed as hell and I don't blame you. It was a bad fucking choice to hide the truth at the bar but I'm hoping you'll let me explain."

Her scoff says it all, especially with the addition of an exaggerated eye roll. Lark continues standing silently otherwise.

"Alright, I guess it's a start that you're still here and not running the other direction. It's hard for me to explain why I feel so demanding and got that upset about him putting his hands on you. In my mind, I see us trying to work this out between us but pretty sure you're on a different page. I wasn't prepared to see you with another man." The words taste bitter on my tongue but I'm trying to be honest. I stare into her honey gaze and hope she lets me in.

Lark tilts her head as she squints at me. "I'm a free agent, Casper. I don't do relationships and I don't get tied down. Not sure what you're planning in your head," she gestures near my temple, "but there isn't much to work out here. I'm not looking for anything more than a night of fun."

A painful spasm attacks my sternum. This isn't the girl I met all those years ago. "What happened, Lark? I asked you once if you believed in destiny and soul mates. Back then, I was pretty sure we agreed on that. What changed your mind and turned you into this . . ." I can't find the right words as my hand is wildly waving up and down her artificial appearance. She might look sexy as fuck but it's a disguise and I want to know why she's hiding.

She lets her arms unwind so she can point at me while fire flashes in her eyes. "You happened to me, jackass. With all your sweet charm and gorgeous blue eyes and promises of getting to know me. Fuck you and your bullshit lies."

"Fuck me, Vix? Shit, I've been a jackass but give me a chance. I need to know if you still feel it, Sweetheart. That deep ache inside that only one person can fill. The need to find all-encompassing love that will change your life. That unbreakable bond between two destined souls. Sound familiar?" I take a few steps toward her as the pressure in my chest increases.

"You make me so mad I could punch you." Her small hands are balled into fists and I wonder if she'll actually take a swing. "I refuse to give you that satisfaction though. I promised myself I wouldn't lose my head over you again but you've already managed to piss me off this much. I don't need to hear your bullshit love lines."

I stalk closer and Lark backs up until she's against the door. It gives me the opportunity to crowd her space without her being able to escape. Thanks to her ridiculously tall fuck-me heels, I don't have to crouch down to meet her eyes.

Only a foot separates us when I ask, "Why did you need to promise that?"

"You know why." She shoots back.

"Do I really? You won't give me the time of day unless I agree to sleep with you. There hasn't been much willingness on your part to shed light on what the hell happened over the last seven years."

Lark glances away but quickly locks her glare back on my face. "As if you want anything else from me, Rowen. I'm just playing the game and keeping my heart out of it. This is me now and the girl I used to be is long gone." She places her hand on my chest before stroking the fabric of my shirt. If she's trying to distract me, her technique is working because I'm already picturing her legs wrapped around my waist while I push her up against the wall.

My willpower is weakening around the edges as her tongue licks along her bottom lip. When Lark lets out a fake-ass moan, I snap out of my lust-fueled trance and see her ploy for what it is.

I snag her arm that's between us before interlocking our fingers and holding them against the cool door. I notice a small tattoo on her wrist and get lost in the simple design for a moment. The tiny heart looks so lonely by itself and I want to know more about it. As I lean closer to ask, the little vixen arches into me, which causes another flash of distracting uncertainty—but I'm not ready to give in.

"What are you trying to prove with this act you're putting on?"

"It's not an act."

"Bullshit, Vix. Tell me the truth."

"As if you deserve it, *Casper*." She says the ridiculous nickname with a sneer.

I don't let her attitude dissuade me.

"Tell me," I whisper across her lips.

Lark shivers before responding. "I want to leave you waiting in the dust, just like you did to me."

I'm startled by her response and unsure if she's joking, but I'll play along. "Just like that? Without finding out if there's any truth behind my 'bullshit love lines'? You'd fuck me and take off?"

She smirks and says, "Absolutely. It will be a night you'll never forget, if that helps sway your decision. I'll do anything you want." Her sultry promise speaks straight to my cock but my heart is still controlling my brain.

I shake my head sadly. "Nah, Vix. You're tempting me, that's for sure. But you mean a lot more to me than that. Hopefully one day you'll feel the same about me."

Lark raises a brow while tipping her chin higher. "Not likely but nice effort. You'll give up soon enough. No man denies sex. Especially when the woman is *very* willing."

"I can be patient and hold out for you to believe again. I've already waited this long."

Her eyes shine with distrust as she squints at me. "Alright, maybe I'll make you fall in love with me first before I abandon ship." Lark's voice reflects humor but little does she know, I'm already falling hopelessly for her.

"I'm already all in, Sweetheart. If that involves you taking off, I'll be sure to follow. No matter what, I want to give this a real shot this time. I thought that was pretty clear." My lips softly brush the corner of her mouth and she turns her head for more contact but I shift my touch closer to her ear. My sight catches on her wrist again and the ink provides an opportunity to turn this conversation around.

"Tell me about your tattoo, Vix."

She veers away as my words reach her but Lark still answers.

"Just a stupid mistake," falls from her painted pout.

Not good enough for me. "Why the outline of a heart?"

"Why the hell not?" She snaps after my nose gently rubs along her pierced lobe.

"Does it have significance or do you just like the symbol?"

Lark spats her response over my shoulder. "It reminds me that my heart is empty. Satisfied?"

A humorless chuckle rumbles from me. "Hardly but it's clear you're done talking about it. Do you trust me, Vix?"

She huffs loudly. "Not even a little bit."

"Why?" I pull away slightly to look at her gorgeous face.

Lark rolls her eyes before snipping back, "Are you serious right now?"

"As a heart attack."

"*Urgh*, I freaking hate that saying. Why does it have to be a heart attack? Those are tragic."

I can't help but chuckle at her remark. "Focus, Lark. We can discuss my vocabulary choices later. Why don't you trust me, Sweetheart?"

A frustrated grumble surges past her lips before she clenches her eyes tightly shut and vigorously shakes her head. If I didn't have her pressed up against the door, I'm sure she'd be stomping off in a flurry right about now.

Lark gives another toss of her wild blonde locks before refocusing her turbulent ambers on me. "You really know how to push my buttons and get my blood boiling. Trust is something you earn or deserve. You don't necessarily have to work hard in order to get it but you do have to be around and actually give a shit though. You definitely don't disappear without a trace, never to be heard from again. Please give me one decent reason why I would ever trust you?"

She pauses for a beat before jumping back in. "Actually no, scratch that. I don't need your pitiful excuses or blabbering. You need to accept that there is no trust between us and there never will be." Lark's breath rushes out of her as she finishes that last statement.

"I came back for you. Several times actually." I blurt without much thought.

Lark's body suddenly locks up and tenses against me. Her facial features appear frozen and she doesn't breathe for several long seconds. I'm slightly concerned by her reaction and lack of snarky response but I give her a few more moments to rally. With a slight wobble of her head and a couple slow blinks, she seems to snap out of it. A quiet questions wheezes out of her parted lips.

"What did you just say?" Her voice sounds stunned and scratchy.

"This is not a discussion I want to have in a storage closet." I reply, hoping we can steer the subject back to safer ground.

Instead, my words appear to infuse Lark with the strength needed to wake up from the stupor she's caught in. "I'm so sorry to inconvenience you but you're the one who dragged me in here. I'm fine not talking at all." Her signature sass is back in full force.

Give the lady what she wants, right?

"Fine. I'm more than ready to tell my side, even in here. You don't know everything that happened when we first met and several instances afterward."

She's listening intently, with her eyes wide and fixed on me, so I keep going.

"When I came into your restaurant that day, I was on a week-end pass from my command post in Tennessee. My entire extended family was having a reunion and I managed to get time away to attend. Long story short, while I was sitting on that patio waiting for you, my commanding officer called with orders to get my ass on a plane back to installation immediately. When they tell you to haul ass, you start running or fucking prepare for serious ramifications." Words get stuck on my tongue because guilt still gnaws at me for leaving without a goodbye.

I rub my thumb along her palm then rest my forehead against her neck, soaking in the comfort of her touch. At least she's here with me now. When Lark clears her throat, it jostles my head so I straighten and finish my story.

"I didn't just race out of there without at least trying to find you. I went inside and looked around but you were nowhere to be found. While I waited near the front doors, my C.O. called again with my departure information and made sure I was on my way to the tarmac. I didn't have a moment to spare and I've been filled with regret ever since, Vix. You changed my life that day and I walked out on you."

Lark starts to interrupt but I'm not quite done. I bring my free hand up to her face and gently swipe along her rosy cheek. "Shhh, Sweetheart. I'm sure you're eager to read my ass the Riot Act but let me say my piece."

She rolls her eyes but nods so I continue.

"I wasn't able to get back to Minnesota for six months, for several reasons, but one of the first stops I made was Brack's Box. You weren't working and the manager wouldn't tell me your schedule. I checked back multiple times over the two days I was in town but didn't have any luck. That didn't mean I'd given up on finding you though.

"The next chance I got to take leave was right before my first deployment and I came looking for you. When I walked into the restaurant and asked for you, the guy manning the front station wondered what I wanted to talk to his girlfriend about. Those words nearly ripped me in half but I figured you must be doing alright without me. I left and didn't come back. I tried to forget about your brilliant brown eyes and bashful smile but I never did . . ." I'm gazing into those same bronze irises as my voice trickles off in that last statement. My heart is pounding against my ribcage, threatening to crack bone, as I wait for her response.

"And here we are now."

"Why should I believe you, Casper? Not gonna lie, your track record isn't stellar. I haven't heard a peep since that massive flower delivery and those cryptic last words you parted with . . ." Lark speaks and her tone is hesitant, which has an ache spreading deep in my gut. She takes a deep inhale, as if to gain momentum, so I jump in before she gets rolling.

"Sweetheart, there was nothing I could do about leaving abruptly that day. Trust me when I say that taking off without letting you know was the last thing I wanted. If I could go back and change anything, the way that day turned out would be at the top of my list. This past week, I was giving you space because I upset you by dropping by unexpectedly. But don't think for a second my silence meant I was giving up. It's the total opposite. I'm coming for you, Vix." My focus latches onto her plump lips while I imagine sucking that pillowy flesh into my mouth. I rock against her before I'm able to stop myself.

Her sharp laughter bursts the moment I thought we were having. "You're barking up the wrong tree with that nonsense. I don't do commitments and I'm not searching for love anymore." A layer of vulnerability colors her speech even though she's putting up one hell of a front.

I poured my truth all over the floor and she's dodging it. Lark is acting tough as fucking nails but I'm confident she wants me to chase her.

Fucking mind games.

I'm planning my next method of attack when Lark's vixen comes back out in full force.

"Are we done here? I have a drink to get back to and the night is still young." Her tone is dripping with suggestion.

"What are you planning for the rest of the evening?"

Lark's hand that's not trapped against the wall maneuvers between us and she walks her fingers up my stomach. Her voice is a purr as she utters, "I'm looking for some company. Pretty sure Ronny is a willing participant if I can't interest anyone else."

My hackles rise as she cranks up her wicked ploys. This woman fights fucking dirty and it's beginning to really bother me. Protective instincts radiate throughout my entire body until everything within me is coiled tight. I push Lark even harder along the door so she's able to tell how tense she's making me. Then I snatch her wandering palm and pin that wrist to the door as well.

Leaning into her, so hardly any space separates us, I murmur across her succulent mouth. "I'll take care of you and will handle your needs from now on. No more other guys. No more dates. No more hook-ups. You need to feel good or want some attention, call me and I'll be there. All you need to do is let your guard down and give me a chance."

"Whatever, Casper. You're delusional. You can't lay your claim on me and expect me to be all right with it. I can handle myself just fine. We won't be anything other than fuck buddies, scratching a carnal itch, if you're willing. Why can't this just be a bit of fun between adults?" Steely resolve flows from her but I hear the slight tremble as she spews more outrageous lines my way. Then her eyes slide away from mine to focus on a spot over my shoulder.

I rest my stubbled cheek against the velvety skin of hers before whispering more truth. "Vix, you don't understand yet but one day it will be crystal clear. There is nothing to claim because you're already mine. You've always been mine. It just took a while for me to find you again."

Lark scoffs and tries to wriggle away but I have her pinned. She stops fighting to say, "If you hadn't left in the first place, you wouldn't have *lost me*." Her fingers move slightly along the wall as if making air quotes. " . . . and we wouldn't be having this stupid argument." The sexy vixen begins struggling against me again, which has my cock painfully hard and ready for what she's offering.

Her frustration is palpable as her tiny body practically vibrates and her fists shake along the door. "Who do you think you are, Rowen? You can't just waltz into my life and start barking orders. You have no right or authority over me. There is no reason for me to listen to this. Now if you'll excuse me, I have a date to get back to."

Those words make me hot for an entirely different reason as flames of fury race up my limbs. This woman is making frantic anger rise to the surface and burn my skin. I quickly release one of her wrists so I can slam my open palm on the wood beside our heads. The sound causes Lark to startle and leap against me. Fucking deserves it for that bullshit act.

"*Goddammit*, Lark! Now you've pushed me too far. I've been trying to stay calm and positive but there are limits. Open your eyes and your ears. You. Are. Mine. If you think I'm going to let you stomp back out there and resume half-ass flirting with that limp dick, you're sorely mistaken. We can do this the easy way or the hard way. I'd prefer us walking out of here together but that's just me. I'm more than willing to take the hard way too." Panting breaths escape me as I try to calm my wildly racing heart.

Lark looks remorseful as she winces and darts her eyes around, searching for a safe spot to look. She clears her throat and asks, "And what might that involve?

I don't hesitate before saying, "Me tossing you over my shoulder and carrying you straight out of here."

That causes her wandering gaze to fix back on me. "You wouldn't dare."

"You've been testing my tolerance plenty, Sweetheart. I'm ready to snap so try me." I lean impossibly closer so my lips brush against hers when I harshly whisper, "I dare you."

Her glare can only be described as ferocious—like she's stabbing me repeatedly with little blades. "I hate the feeling of letting you win but I'm not excited by the idea of being dragged out of here kicking and screaming. I have limits too." She huffs before adding, "I can walk, thank you very much. I won't be in need of your caveman transportation today."

The possessive fury cools immediately once she agrees to leave. Tranquility washes across my heated flesh as I take a much needed sigh of relief. I release Lark's other wrist before backing away from her.

"Good choice. Now get moving."

Lark squeaks in outrage and parks her fisted hands on her hips. "Stop telling me what to do!" She stamps her fancy shoe, like a spoiled brat. "I'm going home and you better not follow me." Then she spins around before flinging the door open, giving me a final glare over her shoulder.

I shake my head while glancing at the ceiling, silently asking for patience. "Wouldn't dream of it, Sweetheart, but you better believe I'll be texting you later to make sure you made it back safely."

She's worth any battle or argument—the peaceful swirling deep in my gut is proof of that. After getting shoved through a metaphorical meat grinder by that combative conversation, a sense of floating euphoria still manages to lifts me up. We are destined to be together, I believe that now more than ever. And oddly enough, I'm glad we hashed it out because clarifying light now shines on the gap currently separating us.

Lark is seeking vengeance for the scorned girl of her past while I'm determined to show her the possibilities of our future. Hopefully we'll both make it out unscathed.

NINE

Lark

'm staring into my cup of coffee, expecting answers to magically appear within the dark brown liquid. I woke up feeling rotten, which wasn't due to the entire bottle of red wine consumed immediately after getting home. Last night with Rowen was an epic disaster and regret has been ricocheting through my skull since I left the bar.

What the hell is wrong with me?

This outrageous plan for revenge against him is turning me into a manipulative bitch and I took it too far yesterday. I'm a mental health professional yet can't fix my own form of instability. Dangling another man in front of Rowen's face after he'd confessed all that sweet stuff makes another bout of nausea churn in my stomach. I'm not cruel or combative—confrontation of any kind usually doesn't sit well with me—but Rowen brings out a psycho side I didn't know existed.

Whenever I lay eyes on him, all common sense flies out the window and I become an unpredictable ball of crazy. I'm always on the defensive around men but it's an entirely new level with Rowen. He makes me want to unleash all the hurt I've experienced even though he doesn't deserve the entire blame. These are truths I'm all too aware of but the games are still being played.

Frustration and pain have been bottled up too tight and I've finally loosened the lid, but a waterfall of emotion threatens to burst out rather than a slow leak. I'm completely mixed up and acting like a wacko who can't control herself. Indecision so dense is clogging my mind and making dizzy. My forehead hits my palm before I tightly clutch my head.

I'm officially losing my marbles.

If Rowen's story about coming back for me is true, my wrath toward him is unwarranted and makes this ridiculous mess more complicated. He was telling me everything I'd wished for, and I wanted to believe every word he was saying, but years of emotional ruin and damage don't erase overnight.

My diva act was way over the top though. When I was spitting those nasty lines at him, my soul was cracking but the storm kept brewing. I probably could be nominated for an Oscar based on my overly dramatic portrayal of a crazy ex-girlfriend scorned one too many times. Chloe, Faith, and Willow would have been cackling in the corner, enjoying the show, no doubt about it.

My psychological flaws were visible like physical scars and I bared them for Rowen to see. He had the chance to run scared like the rest but he didn't budge. Even as I stabbed him with my words and attempted to push him away, he stuck around and kept sparring with me. It makes me think Rowen might understand me.

Yeah, right.

What actually happened was Rowen's face locking up tight as his eyes filled with disappointment. That look caused searing agony to rip through me but I had to protect myself. The threat of potential deception from men is anchored deep within me and pessimistic voices always pester me to shove any guy away—the harder, the better.

He's a liar.

He'll leave again.
He's going to break you.
He just wants to win.

My fucked up mind had been fighting for control while Rowen served me missing pieces from the past. I almost gave in until he pulled that brutish behavior and forced me to snap out of it. My already wavering resistance took another direct hit when I witnessed that commanding version of him. Rowen's soft and romantic side spoke to my heart and melted thick layers of frosty ice shielding it. Then he switched into alpha-male mode, which damped my panties faster than I could comprehend.

He really might be the entire package . . .

Maybe I can end this defective cycle and try again with him. Putting myself out there and on the line is terrifying but Rowen could be worth it. Going on a date wouldn't be horrible and perhaps I could lure him in that way. I bang my already pounding head on the table for taking such a sharp turn.

Lure him?! What the hell am I thinking?

The trickery slithers around in me like an inky fog and my mood plummets when I imagine pushing his buttons in such a vindictive way. Misery replaces any arousal I was infused with moments ago. No matter how much I believe this guy hurt me, serving it back to him doesn't seem feasible without risking my integrity or sanity.

I should back away slowly and cut my losses. I'll keep my dignity, or what's left, and Rowen can have the power of knowing he defeated me. Maybe we could be just . . . nope. Not even going there. We can't be friends. *Period.* I simply refuse to entertain the idea. I doubt Rowen would be interested in being my platonic pal either. There is no denying the insanely intense chemistry buzzing between us—so forceful it's like static zapping along my skin whenever he's close.

I'm so effing confused.

Rowen is impossible to resist, especially with the insta-crazy-love surging through every fiber of my deprived self. Would it be so horrible to surrender and see what happens? The tiny, microscopic piece of my heart that still believes in a happily ever after begins fluttering wildly at the idea. If given the opportunity, that part would spread like wildfire and easily takeover since desperation for true devotion is still very present within me. Faith in love still exists within me, no matter how hard I've tried beating it down and out after getting nothing but rejection. If I give power to hope, possibility, chance . . .

It's only a setup for inevitable pain. A disaster waiting to happen with me standing right in the way.

I'm yanked out of my internal Tilt-A-Whirl when my phone dings with a notification alert. A flurry of butterflies take flight in my belly at the thought of the message being from Rowen. I groan loudly before scrubbing my fingers down my face. These are the types of optimistic ideas that will get me in trouble.

When I glimpse at the screen and see Willow's name, those pesky feelings of possibility fall flat. I try not to let disappointment take shape, but a small knot tightens in my chest regardless.

Freaking Casper.

Using that nickname for Rowen lifts my spirits a tiny bit as I read her text.

> *Willow: Can you help with wedding stuff today? I could really use an extra set of hands.*

This is exactly the type of distraction I need.

> *Me: Count me in. You know I'm always happy to help. Should I come by your house?*

> *Willow: Yes. Perfect. Around 1?*

Me: I'll be there.

That gives me plenty of time to go for a run, reset my toxic brain, and get ready for the day. Then I'll be prepared for whatever love-infused project my friend has lined up.

WHEN WILLOW'S DOOR swings open, I expect to see my friend's smiling face. That's not what happens. The very last person I anticipate greets me. And I shouldn't be surprised in the slightest considering my twist of luck with this guy lately.

Rowen's lips tip up in a blinding grin while I'm sure my mouth is gaping open in stunned shock. "Hey Vix. Fancy seeing you here. What's up?" He leans casually against the wood frame as though we're going to have a nice chat, right here and now.

What the hell is happening? Am I in the Twilight Zone?

It takes a few more moments for the bewilderment to wear off and my heart to resume beating at a normal rate. I continue silently staring at Rowen like he's a mirage and will suddenly vanish in a puff of smoke. When he straightens his stance and chuckles loudly, I begin to believe he's actually standing in front of me.

"Look like you've seen a ghost, Vix. Casper, right? Figured by now you'd be used to seeing me around. Are you coming in or what?"

My mental capacity finally clicks back together. "Why are you here, Rowen? And why are you answering the door like you're living here? Where's Willow?" My questions bang out like rapid gunfire but confusion is still swirling around me.

He doesn't miss a beat. "Willow invited me over. She needs help with something. I just got here and was still at the door when you knocked and figured I'd let you in. Is that all right?"

This entire situation reeks of savvy scheming and my suspicion is confirmed when my friend bounces up next to him. "Lark! There you are. Isn't it great that Rowen could be here too?" She bats her ridiculously long eyelashes at me in a very obnoxious manner before sending a smirk his way.

Little traitor set me up.

I begin moving away from them with my palms raised defensively in front of me. "Listen here you two. I don't know what's going on but I want no part of it. I came over to help you," I point an accusatory finger at Willow, "with wedding stuff and I highly doubt Rowen signed up for that. I'm just going to leave." I take one more step back before Willow grabs me and begins dragging me into her house.

"You're already here so don't be silly. We can get the invitations done even faster with three of us. Win-win! I already have all the materials set up on the table so go sit down." She's talking so fast I'm barely able to keep up but I get the gist. This is happening and Willow isn't taking no for an answer. She releases my wrist and turns to face me.

I'm busy rubbing at my tender skin when I respond. "Fine but I see what you're doing and I'm very disappointed in you."

Willow rolls her eyes and snorts. Rowen approaches and stands next to her. It's clear they've formed an alliance—them against me and I'm outnumbered.

How bad could it possibly be?

Assembling invites won't take long and then I'll beat cheeks out of here. Win-win my ass but whatever.

I swerve around them without further debate and settle into a waiting chair. Rowen takes a seat across the table and his heated gaze sears into me. My face flushes and it seems like the thermostat got cranked up a thousand degrees. I won't get anything done if he keeps looking at me that way.

"What are you staring at?"

"The most beautiful woman I've ever seen."

My breath hitches but I cover it with a huff. "Nice line, Casper."

"When are you going to believe me?" His blazing blue eyes continue devouring me and my blush intensifies under his scrutiny.

Where the hell is Willow?

I clear my suddenly desert-dry throat. "We don't need to revisit this topic so soon. Pretty sure we discussed my lack of faith in you plenty last night."

"I am so fucking sorry about the past. You have no idea how many nights I've stayed awake wondering about you and obsessing over the way that day ended. The guilt has been eating at me ever since." He takes a deep breath. "Give me a chance, Vix. You have to let me earn your trust back." His tone is soft and warm and I want to snuggle up with it. But I can't.

My eyes focus on the piles of colorful paper in front of me. "I'm a mess, Rowen. I drag around a lot of baggage and it isn't easy for me to forget the emotional damage I've endured. And I don't mean from you." I blow out an exasperated breath because I'm starting to sound pitiful. "There has just been a lot of crap without any reprieve so I stopped trying. You're really wasting time asking me for more because I don't have it in me."

He reaches for my hand and intertwines our fingers. "You're so special to me, Sweetheart. I need to show you that. All I want is a shot to prove my feelings. I know you're not immune to the connection between us." Rowen squeezes his grip and the already pleasurable sparks within me thrum even deeper. "I notice your breathing accelerating and your pulse is going crazy. Stop fighting me."

"I'm scared of commitment. Like serious attachment issues. I won't give you the chance to break me again." I whisper while my sight locks on our joined palms.

"Look at me, Vix." I glance up from under my lashes. "One date. Dinner tonight. Forgive me so we can start over."

This guy can battle with the best of them. I tried every tactic in my expansive collection to wiggle away and he isn't backing down. My restraint is crumbling. Leftover confusion from this morning weighs me down as I straddle the line, swaying each way before tipping over. I bite down on my bottom lip and decide to take the leap.

I nod my head slightly while mumbling, "All right."

Rowen's resulting smile is massive and lights up his features. That expression alone makes joy spread through me like warm honey. My choice was the right one. A giddy-grin stretches my lips and we keep staring at each other until everything else fades away. I get lost in his hypnotic ocean eyes as the calm waves soothe my restless soul.

"All right! Did you guys get everything taken care of?" Willow barges into the room and pops our bubble of bliss. She glances at Rowen before looking my way, and then zooms in on our clasped hands. An all-knowing smirk lifts her mouth as she cocks a teasing brow my way. I try to untangle my fingers from Rowen's hold and he grasps me tighter. I huff and puff for a moment before relenting.

"Yeah, yeah. Your little meddling-matchmaker plan worked. Now can we get started on these," I indicate the stacks of craft materials with my free hand, "or was the entire afternoon a ploy to set us up?" I ask, with hints of my typical sass.

Willow tosses her head back to laugh like an evil genius. When she levels her gaze at me again, her green eyes are sparkling with mirth. "I don't know what you two are waiting for. Couldn't you talk and construct at the same time?" Another chuckle bubbles out of her as she takes the chair next to mine. "But really, Lark. I'm glad you see the light."

Her face is so open and honest, I can't stay mad at her. Especially when I'm secretly pleased about her interfering.

TEN

Rowen

I pull into Lark's apartment complex and search for a space big enough to fit my truck. Downtown parking is not meant for vehicles this big but the effort for this evening is fucking worth the headache. It was an entirely different battle earlier while trying to convince my date I should pick her up at all. Thankfully Willow stepped in, again, and vouched for me not being a creepy stalker.

When Willow and I blindsided Lark this afternoon, there was a decent amount of concern knotting my stomach over how she'd react. My accomplice assured me it would all work out, but when it comes to Vix, I'd prefer having more solid ground. There are far too many uncertainties since we don't actually know each other that well. I don't know most of Lark's likes and preferences yet, but I hope to start chipping at the mystery tonight.

I press the buzzer for 5C and wait for Lark to release the lock. A static voice comes from a little speaker near the rows of buttons.

"Hey. I'll be right down."

Is she kidding me?

I press the intercom and respond, "Let me in, Vix. I'm picking you up at the door, just like I told you." I swear a little scoff travels down the line before a loud whir fills the lobby.

By the time I'm on the fifth floor and approaching her place, it's clear Lark is already waiting in the open doorway. This woman enjoys testing me but there isn't much she can do at this point that would scare me off. She's tried plenty of tricks, but I'm still here. I take a deep inhale to ease the nerves tightening my muscles before stepping in front of her.

The calming strategy was pointless because the sight of Lark up close takes my breath away, amongst other things. She has me regretting foregoing some self-love before leaving my house—I'm painfully hard from just one glance. The little vixen stands in her entryway as I devour every inch of her sexiness, innocently unaware of how deep my affection already goes.

Lark's gleaming brown eyes are lined with black, which makes their amber color pop even more. Her shiny blonde hair is pinned up in a complicated twist and a twinge of disappointment pinches at me. Easily running my fingers through her loose strands will be difficult later—but I can always remedy that.

Her lips are painted bright red and look wet from gloss. They're like a flashing flare drawing me in and I'm desperate for a taste. By the end of tonight, I'll have that ruby stain smeared all over my mouth like a trophy. I can't fucking wait to suck all that color from her delectable pout.

As my slow gaze continues down her body, I notice Lark is wearing her trademark silky dress and fuck-me heels. The combination is lethal to my resolve and the seemingly idiotic rules about waiting for sex. The more I stare, the harder it gets to imagine walking away at the end of the night. Thankfully the top of her dress isn't the daringly low style she typically wears so her glorious rack is covered. If it weren't, we might be skipping dinner altogether.

But then she turns around to pull the door closed and lock it.

I almost pass out from the lack of blood flow to my brain.

Pretty sure I sway on my feet and almost swallow my tongue at the sight of her completely bare back. Her naked skin calls to me, from her neck all the way to her ass. All I can do is gawk like a pubescent virgin getting his first glimpse at a woman.

Somehow I find my voice and choke out, "Trying to get me thrown in jail, Vix?"

"What do you mean?" She asks over her shoulder while raising an inquisitive brow.

"Don't bullshit me, Sweetheart. I know you checked out that fine ass of yours in the mirror. I'm going to kill anyone that dares to look at you twice. And in that outfit you're guaranteed plenty of leers." I run my hand over my mouth and groan into my palm to try easing the tension, but she's too fucking hot.

When Lark turns around to face me again, I'm suddenly able to breathe and regain proper functioning of my mind as some of the heated lust dissipates. The little vixen smirks as she closes the few feet separating us. The scent of lavender and vanilla clings to her, which creates another dose of desperation just begging for a taste.

I suddenly remember her gift waiting in my pocket. The sight of her stunning beauty completely distracted me. I take a small step back before pulling out the small box and handing it to her.

Her face pinches with hesitation. "What's this, Casper?"

"Just a little something that reminded me of you."

She lifts the tiny lid and peers inside before freezing. Hopefully she appreciates the special meaning rather than thinking I'm weird. After a few strained moments, I can't take the silence any longer.

"So, what do you think?" The longing in my voice almost causes me to cringe but I manage to keep a straight face. I'm so desperate for her approval it practically vibrates through me.

Warm brown eyes peer up at me and I swear they're a bit glassy. "Why an arrow, Rowen?" Her question is barely a whisper.

My fingers graze lightly along her tattooed wrist. "To pierce your heart, Vix. Since you've already captured mine. Do you like it?"

Lark nods while keeping me locked in her expressive gaze. She glances back to the necklace before lifting it out of the velvet case. "Will you help me?" Her voice is soft as she signals to the chain's clasp.

She twists around and I place the silver strand around her neck, thankful her hair is already out of the way. Lark plays with the charm before setting her heated stare back on me. She moves into my chest with liquid grace and her body melts against me. I'm burning up with her so close, gazing at me with a mixture of gratitude and hunger.

She bites her bottom lip before quietly murmuring, "I really appreciate the gesture but it doesn't mean I'm ready to give in. I'd like to thank you though."

Her bottomless bronze eyes devour me like I'm all she wants to eat. Fire licks at my skin as my blood keeps boiling hotter in my veins. We need to get out of this cramped hallway before I lose my morals and fuck her against the wall.

Without another word, I snatch her hand and weave our fingers together. I use it to turn us toward to elevator. Lark's soft giggle has me glancing at her from the corner of my eye, only to find her looking right at me.

"What's so funny?" I ask after the elevator doors close and we begin descending to the lobby. The air is charged with electricity that seems to zap along every part of my body.

She hums quietly before murmuring, "You're walking like it hurts." Lark sucks her plump lip between her teeth before glancing down at my obvious erection that's practically reaching out for her.

"You care about my wellbeing, Sweetheart? That's very kind of you." My tone is laced with humor but I'm secretly hoping to rile her up a bit.

She scoffs loudly and tries to yank her hand free. "You're twisting my words, Casper. But if you want some help—"

"I'm perfectly comfortable just holding your hand, Vix. Thanks for the offer though. We're going on a date. End of story."

"If you say so . . ." She lets her sentence trail off like a tease but I'm not taking the bait this time.

As the elevator opens and we head out to my truck, Lark finally asks what I've been waiting to share. "Where are you taking me?"

I just go for it. "Brack's Box."

My arm snaps back when she stops abruptly and I turn slightly toward her. I know she wasn't expecting that based off her slack jaw and wide eyes. Her gaze darts around my face as though searching for something.

After a few moments, she clears her throat and drops her stare. "Why?" She whispers to the ground.

"Well, that's where we met and were supposed to have our first date until I fucked it up. You're giving me another chance so I wanted to make it right. Start over where it began in the first place. Is that alright, Vix?" I keep my voice soft and sweet because this is an important moment.

Lark looks up at me from under her full lashes before nodding. Then the only true smile I've seen from her—the type that reaches her eyes—takes over that tempting mouth. The sight has my soul sighing in relief for the first time in seven years.

$$\gg\!\!-\!\heartsuit\!\longrightarrow$$

"WHEN WAS THE last time you were here?" I ask after we've settled into a booth that keeps Lark's naked back out of sight.

Thank God.

"It's been at least two years, maybe longer. After spending so much time here working, it's not a place I choose to visit. I'm glad to be back though. This was very thoughtful of you, Casper." Her tone is light and she's noticeably softening toward me.

"Are you serious with that nickname?"

"What, you're allowed to call me Vix but I can't return the favor?"

"Casper doesn't seem very flattering."

"Because Vixen is?"

I smirk and nod my head in defeat. "Touché." I love verbally volleying with this woman. Her sass is getting me rock-hard all over again.

We order drinks and some cheese dip—because Lark claims it's the best thing ever—before I reach across the table for her hand. I love the sizzle that zaps through me when our skin connects. It's my new addiction.

"Should we get some first date questions out of the way?"

She arches a delicate brow before responding with a simple, "Sure."

With her foxy ambers locked on me, my heart skips and takes off in a sprint.

Shit, why am I so nervous?

"All right, Vix. What are your interests and hobbies? When you're not working, what occupies your time?"

She giggles and rolls her eyes. "Wow. That's funny. I feel like we should be past all that simple stuff, but I guess we're not."

"Would you prefer to talk about something deeper right off the bat? Where you'd like to get married? How many kids you want?" My tone suggests I'm joking but if she wants to tell me, I won't mind.

Her head is frantically shaking back and forth. "Oh, no. No way. We are so not going there."

I laugh quietly before asking, "Hobbies then?"

Lark bobbles her head back and forth, deciding what to tell me. "I love to run, it quiets my constantly racing mind. Spending time with my friends whenever we find a day that works. Listening to music on a rainy day while sipping a dark beer. Ummm . . . going to the beach, swimming, camping, and tubing." Suddenly her free hand finds my forearm and her nails start gliding along my sensitive flesh. The tingles her touch cause travel straight to my dick and I bite my lip to trap the indecent groan ready to escape. Then the little vixen purrs out, "I enjoy finding male company when the mood strikes." Her voice is dripping with sexual innuendo and promise of dirty fun to follow.

I slam on the brakes before she can lead me any further down this road. As pleasurable as her fingers feel tracing along my skin, I'm not letting her distract me. I snag that wandering hand and hold it too.

"That's definitely stuff we can enjoy together. Those sexy diversion strategies you're using don't belong on our date though. I want the real you. Not the alternate version you've been hiding behind. This,"—I lift our clasped palms—"is different between us. I want all of you, every piece. Once you figure that out, everything will be much easier. You can't dissuade me, Vix." I grin at her when she playful pouts. Lark leans back and averts her gaze, as if lost in thought.

I pull her back up so she's closer before continuing. "Let me in, Sweetheart. I promise this isn't just messing around for me. Can you try trusting me?"

Lark's anxious eyes quickly scan around the restaurant, not focusing on anything. She gulps audibly before finally looking at my face. "I'm scared of being vulnerable," she whispers and I'm sure it takes a lot for her to admit that.

A small smile lifts my lips as she willingly gives me that small piece. "Sweetheart, we'll take it really slow. One day at a time. I'm in no rush. You just need to be willing to give me a shot. Can you do that?" I murmur quietly into the space between us. A huge sigh of relief escapes me when she nods slowly.

The rest of the meal goes smoothly and I learn plenty of random facts about her. Lark's mom still lives in the suburbs, close to where we are now. She has a younger brother that lives in Duluth for college and an older sister that lives in Denver. Her favorite color is pink, tortellini is her pasta of choice, she likes mixed vodka drinks and red wine, dogs are better than cats, and she loves kids—especially the teens she helps through her job.

I tell Lark about my mom and dad that live on the opposite side of the city. She hears about my two younger brothers that go to school in different states. Royal blue is my favorite shade, peanut butter and jelly is the only thing I'm good at making, I'd love to own a dog one day, my "massive" truck is not compensating for anything, and she's the most gorgeous woman I've ever seen. Sworr Security is a topic I spend plenty of time on—I tell her a little about Lincoln too. My time in the army is something I gloss over because it's tough to discuss, which she seems to understand.

Since the evening goes well, I'm confident about getting that goodnight kiss and the bold feeling builds on the drive back to her apartment. The vision of her delectable mouth covering mine causes my foot to press down harder on the accelerator. Lark's lipstick has miraculously remained perfectly in place but I'm ready to remove it.

As we're walking to her door, my hand is on the silky skin of her back while nerves creep in and tie my gut into tight knots. I focus on keeping my palm steady so she doesn't feel the tremble. I'm terrified of screwing this up but I have fate on my side—and hopefully Lark at this point.

She stops and turns toward me in the empty hallway before gripping the front of my shirt in her fist. "Want to come inside for a nightcap?" She murmurs across my jaw after pulling me even closer. Lark's hushed suggestion ramps up the aggressive arousal already pumping through my body and punches enormous holes into my resolve. The desire is almost enough to completely take over the anxiety skittering down my spine.

Focusing on her sparkling amber eyes, I attempt to calm the conflicting emotions and push it all away.

"I'm not giving into you yet, Vix," I lean against her and whisper.

"Oh yeah? Then what do you call this, Casper?" She asks while rubbing against me.

"You giving into me."

A bark of laughter bursts out of her before she takes a step back. "Just because I went on a date with you doesn't mean I'm ready to fall head over heels. I'm still in charge and call the shots. Plus, I was only offering a drink."

Lark still has her guard up but that only means I need to try harder. Maybe getting a taste of her lips isn't the best idea tonight.

"We'll see, Sweetheart. I'm serious about getting to know each other. I mean, you're very tempting but there's other stuff that needs to happen first. I'd love to spend more time with you though, if the offer still stands."

She releases a long sigh before letting me go. When she turns to open the door and I catch sight of her exposed flesh on full display, desire takes the driver's seat and controls everything else. I follow her inside like an eager pig blindly walking to slaughter.

The last of my freshly restored resistance crumbles as the lock clicks shut.

One kiss can't hurt, right?

ELEVEN

Lark

’m heading toward the kitchen when Rowen grabs my arm and spins me back to the entryway. I practically fall into him as we land against the door. My eyes are wide with shock as Rowen wraps his arms around me and pulls me flush against his body. Before I can ask what the hell is happening, his hungry mouth crashes down on mine.

The surprise radiating through my limbs wears off once we're connected and I eagerly open my lips when his tongue requests entrance. Rowen tastes like the spearmint gum he was chewing earlier and the fresh flavor is intoxicating. He dives into my mouth aggressively—like he's lost control and can't get enough—and I suck his tongue hard in response. His hands leave my waist and travel up my back before his fingers spear into my hair.

Rowen uses his grip to tilt my head at an angle he wants and it's clear he's running the show. The move causes thick desire to flood my system. A lusty moan escapes my throat as he sucks my bottom lip into his mouth and bites down softly. My knees threaten to buckle so I lean further into him, thankful Rowen is supported by the door behind him.

His answering groan sounds like a green light for more so I slide my palms down his torso until reaching the waistband of his shorts. My fingers find the zipper as I begin lowering to my knees, but Rowen stops my descent by clutching me tighter.

"No, Vix." His voice is gravely. "That's not what I want. Stay up here." Then he tugs me up so we're facing each other. I wish my heels were off so his direct stare wouldn't be so easily met. Shame consumes me and heats my cheeks and I drop my gaze to the floor.

Almost instantly Rowen murmurs, "Sweetheart, look at me." But I refuse with a shake of my head.

He tries again. "Vix . . ."

The enormous lump clogging my throat won't allow me to speak and tears threaten to fall, but I won't allow them. After taking several deep breaths through my nose, I try to piece my shield back together.

"I was just trying to do something nice for you, so you'd feel good." My meek tone reflects my misery and I feel completely ridiculous. My inner defenses demand my bitter bitch rallies. "Seems like you're not interested. What kind of man turns down a blow job? Am I really that repulsive you won't let my mouth touch your dick?" I wiggle out of his hold and put a foot of distance between us.

"Lark, I care so much about you. Who put these destructive ideas in your mind? It's the complete opposite for me. Have I not made that clear? You're so much more than a quick fuck." His voice is like a dull roar that can't compete with the crashing waves in my warped mind. Only one word stands out. He called me Lark, not Vix.

My ears burn from hearing Rowen use my actual name rather than the silly nickname he's adopted for me. I pretended to hate it, but let's be honest, it made warm fuzzies coat my skin and left my heart beating wildly. It seemed like something special we shared and he just ripped it away.

I slip deeper into dark despair and nasty negativity grasps me. I'm mentally pushing and shoving him away with all my metaphorical might. A choked laugh escapes before I respond with venom lacing my tone. "You'll never get more from me, especially after that rejection shit you just pulled."

Rowen interrupts before I can say more. "I don't need you to suck me off tonight because I'm after far more than that. I want your heart." He lifts an open palm, aiming for my blazing face, but I stepped out of reach.

Pain flashes through his blue eyes, like a lightning bolt piercing the surface of a calm lake. Rowen's tight jaw tics before he growls through clenched teeth, "Don't shut me out and walk away. I can't handle it. I know we share something special and I understand it's my fault you don't trust me. I'm very sorry for the past, Vix. Please believe that I am. But you need to give me a real chance so we can work together on all the other shit." His chest to rises and falls rapidly. "Can you forgive me, Sweetheart? I'm not sure how we'll move forward if you can't."

My eyes narrow into slits as I continue building up the wall separating us. I'm too far gone to evaluate our situation responsibly and humiliation threatens to push me over the ledge. Have I really been that closed off and difficult? Of course I have—that was the entire point. My heart is always on serious lockdown . . .

Shit.

I'm silently hiding years of hurt as I keep lashing out. "You're the one sending fucking mixed messages, Rowen. I wasn't planning anything until you grabbed me. You," I point a trembling finger at him, "made the move. Not me."

He turns away from me to face the door before resting his forehead against the wood. I see the heavy exhale leave Rowen's huge body as he threads his fingers behind his neck. When he straightens and spins back around, his face is relaxed as his light eyes stare deeply into mine. Rowen's genuine gaze softens my hardened edges—just slightly. Then he opens his mouth.

"I shouldn't have done that, you're right. I keep fucking up and it's my fault we're arguing. I can't control myself around you because there's so much want burning inside of me. I wanted to kiss you so badly and didn't think it would escalate so quickly."

What the actual fuck?!

Rowen just took this to an entirely different level. The slim possibility of me escaping the oppressive darkness determined to pull me under evaporates instantly.

The pain must be radiating from my eyes because an apology is already dripping from his lips as he takes a step toward me. "I'm sorry, Sweetheart. *Fuck.* I didn't mean that. This entire conversation has gotten out of hand. Maybe I should go?"

Avoiding his gaze as I whisper, "I thought you liked me?"

Rowen shakes his head slightly as his brows pinch together in confusion. "What? Of course I like you, Vix. I'm just afraid of fucking up even more." His voice is meant to be consoling but I only hear him leaving. Slowly but surely.

He reaches forward to rub my shoulder but I step away and his hand drops limply by his side. I can't feel the pleasurable balm Rowen's soothing touch gives me right now. Not when he's about to leave for good. I officially scared him away and I wasn't even fucking trying anymore.

Dammit.

It's all screwed up now. Rowen is going to go and never come back. I pushed too hard.

Fuck.

Fuck!

My heart is pounding as these thoughts continue spinning faster, down and down they go, until all I hear is the rejection pounding into my skull as the voices hiss victoriously in my ear.

Why would he stay for you?

You're a mess.

You'll never make anyone happy.

He will always leave you.

You'll always be alone.

On a fucking loop, the taunting bangs around my brain. I want to scream and cry but Rowen is still standing in front of me, watching me with that same look of confusion marring his gorgeous face.

I'll miss him but he needs to leave. *Now.* One final shove ought to do the trick. Then I can meltdown in peace.

"Why are you still here?" The misery oozes from my words but I ignore it.

He takes a step closer but I instantly retreat. "Remember the arrow, Sweetheart? You've caught me and I'm not going anywhere. Maybe I'll walk out that door tonight but I'll be back. I want to be here for you, no matter what."

The charm around my neck tingles with his reminder. I bite my tongue to keep my truths buried deep. I attempt to reconstruct my usual detached façade but it's too late. I'm exposed and out in the open with nowhere to hide. The cracks are far too wide and the floodgates are about to burst.

"I need to be alone." I hate the vulnerability that has my voice shaking.

Rowen gives me an overall appraisal before responding. "I can stay, Sweetheart. Maybe we can have that drink after all." He sounds hopeful but I'm sure he's more than ready to get out of here.

I do my best to maintain eye contact while saying farewell to the man I thought was different. "I'm fine. Really. Thank you for tonight. I had a great time." I pray my tone is steady and Rowen won't catch me crumbling, but I hear the wobble clear as crystal.

He nods his head with a sad smirk tilting one side of his lips. "I'll text you later, Vix. Please think about what I've said. " Rowen's voice is hushed and I hold his soulful gaze until he turns to go.

When the door shuts behind him, I tumble into the black abyss as a loud sob shakes my chest. Old wounds rip open as the familiar sting of rejection and doubt pour in. All I want is for Rowen to reassure me that true love fills his heart, *for me*. But I'm fucked up—insecure and damaged—so admitting that deep need is extremely difficult. Apparently I'd rather force an incredible guy out of my life than tell him how I really feel.

I'm so stupid.

Stupid, stupid, stupid!

Each word is punctuated by a slap to my head. The nasty ridicule bashes into me like a semi-truck as tears stream down my cheeks. I cover my mouth with a trembling palm to muffle the uncontrollable wails spilling from my throat. I'm spiraling fast and sure, set on total destruction of any progress I've made over the years.

Loud pounding on the door manages to shatter through the crushing wreckage my mind has become. I lay down on the cold tile and curl into the fetal position while I wait for the banging to stop. Whoever's on the other side will give up soon enough—just like everyone else has.

Except he doesn't.

Rowen swings the door open and strides toward my crumpled form. Just like Prince Charming in all his masculine glory, storming in the save the princess.

I squint through my puffy eyelids, unable to believe he actually came back. Doubt keeps chewing at my stinging skin but then he kneels down and gathers me into his muscular arms.

"I'm here, Vix. I'll always come back."

TWELVE

Rowen

After I stepped into the deserted hallway, I propped my weary body against the wall and took a few moments to extinguish the flames scorching my gut. Lark put up a tough fight to get me gone but I saw right through her act. Those expressive brown eyes were shimmering with unshed tears as her lip wobbled, begging to release a sob.

She asked me to leave so I respected her space and did—but only for a little bit while the dust settles. I'm done messing around and after what just happened, Lark needs me to prove how serious this is. No more skirting around and dodging bullets. We're diving in head first, *together.*

The sound of her crying smashes through the wall and agony stabs at my soul each second I'm not rushing back in there. My little vixen is guarded as hell, for reasons still unknown to me, but I'm prepared to climb any barrier standing in the way. I'm hoping she's ready to break those blocks down. When a garbled wail reaches out from inside, that's my cue go to get my girl.

I knock a few times first and give her the chance to let me in. When nothing but silence greets me, I let myself in. My stomach cramps painfully when I see Lark curled up on the cold floor, with swollen eyes and blotchy skin. I shouldn't have left her but there's no time for regret. I'm here now.

I kneel down before scooping her trembling body into my arms. I pull her tight against me and whisper, "I'm here, Vix. I'll always come back." Then I place a soft kiss on her balmy temple.

Lark doesn't respond as sobs continue shaking her entire form but she grips onto my shirt with fierce strength. I hold her close and let her cry as my eyes fill with tears. "Sweetheart, you're breaking my heart." My throat closes up as a few drops trail down my cheeks. "I'm so sorry I walked out that door. I shouldn't have listened to you."

She sniffles and rubs her forehead along my pec. I'm sure the erratic beat in my chest bangs as loud as a drum. Lark coughs a couple times as she sucks in choppy breaths.

At an almost silent volume she murmurs, "Fitting since you broke mine."

Air gets trapped in my lungs for a few tense seconds and I fear she's about to shove me away. Then she burrows deeper into me while muttering *"I'm sorry"* over and over. I have to blink quickly to rid the moisture that keeps collecting behind my lids but this woman is dragging the sorrow out of me. I'm rocking us gently while shushing softly.

All I can say is, "I'm so fucking sorry, Sweetheart. No more pushing away. This is it now."

Lark nods frantically while yanking me closer with trembling fists. I barely hear the jumbled request when she asks me to stay but her soft words scream at me like they're booming over a loudspeaker.

My response is muted against her hair. "Always, Vix. I'll always stay."

She tilts her chin up and I catch her watery gaze. "Can we go lay down? I won't try anything." Her voice still bounces with uncertainty and I need to put that vulnerability to rest.

A quiet chuckle breaks free, hopefully evaporating the gloomy mood. "Sweetheart, I'm here for you. Whatever you need, whatever you want. Tell me what to do. Everything else will get sorted later. All right?"

She mutters flatly, "Yes. Right."

We untangle our twisted limbs before standing up. Lark is avoiding eye contact and I don't want any shame or embarrassment trying to keep us company tonight. All I want is her.

"Look at me, Sweetheart." It takes a few moments before she complies. "Don't be shy with me. I'm here because you're very special to me. You have been since we first met. Hopefully you'll understand that soon enough."

Lark bites her lip and shuffles her high heels.

"Why do you wear those torture devices? I mean, you're legs look long and sexy as fuck but don't they hurt?" Curiosity has me asking the random questions.

The distraction seems to relax her stiff shoulders as tension seeps out. Lark blows out a heavy exhale while staring down at her shoes. When she looks back at me, there is a little grin lifting her lips.

She shrugs and says, "They make me feel pretty and sophisticated. Once you get used to them, they're actually really comfortable. I prefer wearing a pair of pumps over flats any day."

"I'll take your word for it."

Lark's smile grows wider. "What? You don't want to borrow them?"

If it made her beam at me like this, I probably would, but I'm not about to tell her that. "Nah, Vix. They look far better on you." My hungry eyes soak up every inch of her gorgeous body, slowly and deliberately. I'm sure she's aware of my perusal and hope it boosts her confidence even further.

Pink explodes on Lark's cheeks as she dips her chin, and I

mentally fist pump in victory. When she shyly glances up at me through her lashes, my breathing stalls and my gut clenches. I'm so fucking glad I met this woman.

When she yawns and stretches her neck, I lace our fingers together before nodding toward her bedroom. Her caramel eyes reflect so much relief and appreciation that seeps straight into my protective instincts. All I want is to shower her with love and devotion.

Lark sits on the fluffy mattress and I kneel before her. I run my rough palms down her silky legs, and goose-bumps blossom along her skin. My motives aren't sexual in the slightest—even though my cock is rock fucking solid. A deeply ingrained need to worship her is currently taking control as I carefully slip the heels off Lark's delicate feet.

I gently rub along her soles for a few minutes, making sure my touch is tender yet strong. The lingering tension seeps out of her body and she hums quietly as my fingers continue massaging. I resist the urge needling at me to drift up her legs because mixed messages caused a shit storm I'm not eager to repeat. Instead, I move to the bed and take a seat next to her. Twisting my torso to face Lark, I wait for her to decide what happens next.

Lark silently surveys my face, her eyes scanning over my relaxed features. Even with thick streaks of black makeup staining her cheeks, she's the most beautiful woman I've ever seen. Pure joy tunnels through me that I'm the lucky bastard sharing this moment with her. Lark blows out a fast exhale, causing her puffy lips to buzz loudly.

"So, I'm a mess. Emotionally and physically." A humorless chuckle leaves her. "I'm going to start by cleaning this," she gestures to her face and body, "up so I'll be more comfortable when we talk. Please make yourself at home."

"Take your time, Sweetheart. I'll just hang out until you're ready."

Lark nods before whispering, "Thank you."

She gets up from the bed before walking toward what I assume is the bathroom. Before she disappears from sight, Lark turns back to me. "You have no idea what it means to me that you came back, Rowen. Really and truly. Hopefully I'll be able to explain it one day." Her soft words lift my spirits as the boulder in my gut disappears.

When I'm alone, I stand and stretch the kinks out of my sore muscles. My dick is still half-hard since apparently the no-sex memo is an extremely difficult concept for part of me to grasp in Lark's presence. It hasn't been an issue for a long time but she's detrimental to the restraint I'm attempting to keep in place. Lark has desire constantly throbbing throughout my entire body, making her almost impossible to resist. Our argument earlier reminded me why I'm choosing to wait and reinforced my wavering self-control. Getting between the sheets would only further complicate our fragile status.

I adjust my aching junk and dread the inevitable pain that will soon radiate from my groin. Blue balls suck ass but restoring Lark's faith in me will be worth it. I refuse to ever give off the impression I'm only interested in fucking. We have the rest of our lives to screw like rabbits. For now, I want to discover the truth behind what's holding her back.

As if hearing my thoughts, Lark walks into the room looking like my every fantasy brought to life. Her long blonde hair is loose around her shoulders and her face is wiped clean. She's all natural and fucking stunning. Her lean body is covered by a massive shirt that's several sizes too big and almost touches her knees. An intense wave of jealousy washes over me at the thought it once belonged to another. I tamp down the emotion because she's here with me, no one else. Someday soon *my* shirt will be draped over her delicious curves.

Lark fidgets with the hem and appears nervous again. I'm

unsure how to make this situation more comfortable so I wait for her to take the lead. She glances up at the ceiling before rolling her shoulders and straightening her spine. When her eyes find me again, they're glimmering with determination and confidence.

She clears her throat softly. "I apologize for being a bumbling disaster. What happened out there," Lark points to the hallway, "took a lot out of me. Do you mind if we lie down and talk?"

"Not at all, Vix. Do you want me to sit over there?" I ask while nodding toward a chair in the corner.

"Would you mind lying down with me? Nothing more. I could really use a cuddle."

I immediately open my arms and wave her in. "Come here, Sweetheart."

Lark doesn't hesitate before collapsing into me. Once I've wrapped her up tight against me, she nuzzles deeper into my chest as a huge sigh eases out of her, hopefully in relief.

We remain locked together for a few moments before I begin slowly lowering us to the bed. Once we're situated and resting on her heap of pillows, I pull Lark even closer and press a gentle kiss to her forehead.

"Why are you so wonderful?" She whispers suddenly.

A stunned laugh escapes me. "What do you mean?"

"Everything you do is perfect. I'm terrified to wake up from this dream and find you gone." Her voice trembles slightly and I imagine this being a frequent fear for her, but never again.

I shift and bring my palm up to Lark's smooth cheek, stroking her flawless skin. "I'm right here, Sweetheart. I promise this is real. You'll never have to be without me, if that's what you'd like. That's exactly what I want."

Her cautious gaze plows into my steady stare, reminding me to tread carefully. Lark must find whatever she's searching for because the words start pouring out.

"I don't even know where to start. Everything related to men in my life is a tangled web of bad decisions laced with even worse choices." She pauses briefly, as though collecting her thoughts. "I wasn't lying about my issues with men. My dad walked out on us when I was eleven, without any explanation. One morning he just packed up his shit and took off. My mom was a total wreck at first but managed to bounce back pretty quickly. She's an amazing woman and I wish her strength transferred to me." She's been stroking her fingers along my back but their movement abruptly stops.

"It took a while for his absence to truly impact me. A girl needs her father around to provide unconditional male acceptance, otherwise she'll go looking for it in all the wrong places." Lark's voice trails and I wonder if she's waiting for me to respond.

Just as I'm about to speak, she dives back in. "Maybe I read too many romance novels growing up but finding a boy to love me was all I wanted. After dreaming of Prince Charming sweeping me off my feet as a little girl, I started creating the ultimate guy and kept building him up with each passing year. I wasn't sure any man could meet the standard I set but then you strolled into Brack's Box and changed my life."

The shocked hitch in my breath is completely involuntary but extremely noticeable since Lark is snuggled up real close. She laughs at my reaction before muttering, "Crazy, right? That's only the beginning. My interaction with you increased this radical belief in soul mates exponentially."

I start to interject because *why didn't she say so sooner?* But she cuts me off. "Just let me talk, okay? You're not responsible for the stupid shit I put myself through but for a long while I didn't see it that way. I blamed the hell out of you. *Unfairly.* I can admit that now." She sounds almost sheepish but I'm still stuck on how she must have felt that day we met. Guilt piled on top of guilt weighs me down but Lark is unaware of my internal warfare.

"The desperation to find my one true love got out of control, really fast. No one could stop me and not many even tried. Like my tattoo. I got an empty heart with the crazy goal to fill it in once I found *the one*. My search was nonstop and extremely toxic. It started with me being overly sweet and far too willing to please the guy I was dating. Their interests became mine and I'd do whatever they asked, that sort of thing."

My mind cruelly displays visions of a young Lark doing unspeakable things to these fucking ungrateful little shits. I want to pummel the crap out of each one and force them to apologize while kissing the ground she walks on. I should never have left her. This is entirely my fault . . .

When Lark's hands resume their massage, her touch yanks me away from those dark thoughts—for now.

She yawns but keeps talking. "When that didn't work, I played hard-to-get. I would flirt but let them pursue me. Men like a challenge, right?" She scoffs sarcastically. "I kept putting myself out there like an idiot, only to get rejected again and again. Each time, a new spark of hope would strike. I'd think 'this could be the one' but all I was doing was setting myself up for failure. When you desperately crave that sort of attachment, the error of your ways is pretty hard to see until it's too late. Every disappointment ate away at my tender heart until all that remained was a bitter lump of flesh. My fear of abandonment had morphed into an aversion to commitment. If I didn't give anyone a chance, they wouldn't have the opportunity to leave me. *Win-win.*" Lark's words stab the small gap between us until she tries rolling away. I don't let her get far before she's dragged back into my tight embrace, this time with her ass nestled against my dick.

I rest my cheek against her satin hair before murmuring, "How can you say that? What type of life would that leave you, never experiencing love? I'm so fucking sorry you went through all that without me around, but we can fix it. Just don't shut me out, Sweetheart. Your days of being alone are over."

Lark's eyes are probably rolling while she huffs loudly. "Oh really? You sure as hell couldn't deny me fast enough earlier." Her voice is full of hostility and her body practically vibrates with pent up frustration.

It's time to give her some of my secrets. "Vix, you're so fucking wrong and I can't wait to prove it to you. Let's not jump to conclusions anymore, alright? Let me tell you my shit and we'll go from there." A deep exhale streams out with my story. "So, I was on active duty in the army for eight years and I served two tours overseas fighting for our country. When I was deployed, I watched several of my closest friends die. Experiencing war and that type of trauma makes you appreciate each day you're given. Life is precious and can be over with the pull of a trigger. I'm done throwing time away on worthless shit and have been for a while. I made a promise to myself that the next woman I slept with will be my forever. I've taken that vow very seriously for the last three years."

Lark sucks in a startled breath but I keep going.

"That's why I want to wait, Vix. I'm sure you're not ready for that yet but now you know where I'm coming from. I would love to be buried deep inside you," I rock my hips into her ass so she can feel my eager dick, "but finding my wife first is very important to me. Sex has to be much more intense if there's love between the two experiencing it. I mean, I don't know but I'm ready to find out. When our bodies connect, it's going to blow our fucking minds. The pleasure will be overwhelming. Our souls will join together as our bodies become one." My heart is pounding wildly as I spill my deepest desires.

Only silence greets me and anxiety begins creeping along my skin. Maybe Lark isn't interested in my plan . . .

"Who are you? What type of man talks like this?" She interrupts my worry and relief replaces the nerves.

"I'm yours."

My words seem to please her as a hum rises from her throat. "I feel like you're using the best lines in the book to dupe me into screwing you but I've been practically begging for it and you haven't given in. So, you're actually serious? Three years?"

"As a heart attack."

She groans and shakes her head. "Not that again."

I chuckle softly. "Anymore questions?"

"Just one."

"Let's hear it."

"Will you stay over?"

"Me leaving isn't even an option, Vix."

THIRTEEN

Lark

Why do Monday mornings suck so bad?

Even as a self-proclaimed workaholic, I've always found myself dragging ass at the start of each week. My usual level of loathing is even worse than usual thanks to Rowen and his magical words. He's been busy whipping up a brand-new fairytale for me to fall helplessly in love with, effectively distracting me from reality and piles of paperwork. Regardless of his enchanting persuasion, indecision still swims within the irresistible urge to surrender everything to him.

Can I really trust him?

When Rowen confessed how long he's gone without sex, I almost choked on my tongue in disbelief.

How is that possible?

He's so sexy and handsome. Successful and driven. Plus, he has a way with words that should have a hoard of hussies falling over themselves to get him. It's very possible Rowen has exceeded all the expectations I created once upon a time. He's far superior to any guy I dreamed up—the real Mr. Right ready to sweep me off my feet. I just have to let him.

We've been texting nonstop since he left my apartment yesterday morning and my cheeks hurt from grinning so much. Our banter makes me giggle and swoon, which is another cause for concern. I didn't think this giddy girl existed within me anymore but with each message, another chunk of my resistance dissolves.

His last words were so sweet, I can't help re-reading them as the zero productivity continues.

> Rowen: Is it too early for you to move in with me? Waking up alone blows. Plus, watching you sleep in a huge bonus. Even if you snore. How am I going to last a week without seeing you?

My chest aches at the reminder of his extended absence. Already missing him this much should scare me, but Rowen has made it very clear how much he cares for me. I'm terrified of getting too attached but he easily calms my fears by being overly affectionate. I love it. *A lot.*

I'm finding myself effortlessly swaying toward Rowen as he continues to prove me wrong. My jaded complex about men has held me back but he's given me no reason to hesitate. I'm tired of being closed-off and alone, this frosty attitude is exhausting. Rowen is confirming unconditional love is possible, which is what I've been frantically searching for. So, what the hell is my problem? Why can't I just let go and take the plunge?

I wish this didn't have to be a debate but a lump lodges in my throat as I recall years of emotional anguish. If only time can rewind so we could go back. Rowen's reassurance then would have meant everything to me. Now I'm a scorned woman with a crippled perspective toward relationships. In spite of all that, he's still managing to soften my jagged edges as he seeps through my tough exterior. Rowen could really be the one to fix it after all.

As I'm busy battling my conflicting thoughts, Willow walks by and I call out to her. When she steps into my office, a pleased smirk is already lifting her lips. "Hello to you too. Ready to thank me for getting involved?"

I snort. She's so full of it. "Whatever. You're ridiculous." I'll never admit she was right for forcing my hand but her sneaky move ended up helping. "Speaking of Rowen—"

She cuts me off while sitting down across from my desk. "Who's talking about him? I just wanted a little appreciation for all my hard work." Willow laughs and the pure joy lighting her up is infectious.

My smile spreads wider. "Listen here, there is a reason I wanted to chat. Stop interrupting me with your nonsense. Just hear me out, okay?" She rolls her eyes but motions for me to continue. "Do you believe in soul mates? Like destiny and fate?"

A cackle bursts out of her. I should have known better than to ask. Willow starts flapping her chaps before I can tell her to forget it. "Have you met me? And my fiancé? Lark, you're the one being ridiculous. I believe Xander and I defied the odds stacked against us but I give credit to something beyond our control too. Not only were we separated and suffering, but we had to keep fighting for our happily ever after."

Willow ditches the goofy attitude and gets more serious as her stare lasers into me. "I still think about the moment Xander showed up at my house. I couldn't believe it. I'd described the neighborhood a few times during random conversations and maybe mentioned my address, but there was no way I expected him to come find me. How is that possible? When I asked him, Xander told me he just knew—like this crazy gut-feeling deep inside. He had to find me and there was a driving need pushing him. It didn't hurt that he gave the truck driver my general location based off memory but it's more than that. You know? There is a greater power at work and I absolutely believe that." Her soft voice is bursting with a sense of wonder and trust that captivates me. I want to believe so badly.

We sit together in silence while I determine what to divulge.

Obviously there's a reason I asked and she's not going to walk out of here without knowing why. I fidget and fuss with my hair to keep occupied while Willow continues to patiently wait me out. Finally I blow out a heavy exhale and decide to go for it. Desperation to get this weight off my shoulders practically forces the words from my mouth.

"I think Rowen is the one," gets blurted far too loudly for the small space we're in. And after taking a much needed breath to calm the eff down I add, "I mean, I really like him. He's so perfect, all the time. How can he be so amazing and single? I don't get it. And why me? I'm such a basket case. I've sworn off finding a guy to settle down with and then Rowen stomps back into my life. I think it's time to try again." My lungs are burning from oxygen deprivation as my eyes cloud over with unshed tears.

Shit, this can't happen at work.

Willow reaches forward and grabs my hand, giving it a quick squeeze before releasing. Her comfort makes me want to cry for a totally different reason.

Why am I such a train wreck?

She interrupts my mini-meltdown with some sound advice. "Want to know what I think?" I'm nodding manically before she finishes the question. "I'm not about to sing but sometimes you have to just *let it go* by trusting in destiny. Let blind faith lead the way and take a chance. There will always be crap to get over because life isn't meant to be simple. Finding true love is worth it."

I haven't told Willow enough about my disastrous dating history for her to understand why that isn't so easy for me. She's right though. If I want the ultimate reward, there will be a decent amount of risk. Rowen is different than any dumbass from my past and I need to get over the assumption he's going to leave me. It's time to trust again.

After swallowing the lump of emotion in my throat, I'm ready to respond. "Thank you, Willow. I needed to hear all that.

You're a really good friend. And I'm sorry about all this," I wave a hand around my face, "craziness. Maybe I'm coming down with something." I attempt to keep my tone light but nerves are skittering up my back. I'm going to give Rowen a chance but it still scares the hell out of me.

Willow chuckles while raising a questioning brow. "The only thing you're sick with is L-O-V-E." Apparently she feels the need to spell it out.

I scoff to hide my truth. "Let's not go too far. Who knows if he even *really* likes me." I'm lying through my teeth but she doesn't know that. Rowen has made it clear that he wants *everything* to do with me.

Now it's Willow's turn to huff. "Okay, Lark. You're the queen of being guarded and you'd never ask me about soul mates if Rowen wasn't interested. You're so full of bologna." Her typical sass is back with an added smirk.

My skin is getting itchy with her attention locked on me so I change the subject. "Enough about me, Future Mrs. Dixon. Anything new with wedding plans?" We talked about her upcoming nuptials in great depth a few days ago but this is a foolproof way to get Willow off my case.

"Not really. I talked to Wren yesterday and she promised to be here. Rodeo season or not. She can't come to the bachelorette party but that's expected. You're coming though, right? It's only a few of us but you're my only other bridesmaid so you better show up." She switches topics without batting a perfect eyelash.

Willow's question has my face heating as I recall Rowen asking me something related to that night as well. Of course she notices. "Why are you blushing, Lark? You better not be planning to have a stripper show up." She holds up her palms, as if that will stop me from inviting naked men to her house. "Xander will be there and I'm not interested in getting a lap dance. Please tell me you followed my carefully laid out, strict instructions."

"Wow, thanks for the vote of confidence. Bridezilla much?" I lift a snarky brow her way. "Rowen asked me to be his date. That's it. Satisfied?" My bridezilla comment goes right over her head since she's focusing on the mushy part.

Go figure.

Willow starts bouncing in the chair while clapping her hands like a child with a sugar-high. "Oh my gosh, you two are totally going to do it!"

"Seriously, Willow? *Do it?* You can't even say sex?"

"Quit being—"

She stops mid-sentence as Cindy, the director around here, pokes her head into my office. Her beautiful gray eyes seek out my friend. "Hey Willow. Sorry to barge in but there is a parent here to see you." Then she disappears from sight. That's how our boss works, fast and efficient.

Willow stands and starts walking out but pauses before reaching the door. She glances back over her shoulder and says, "Don't think I missed that bridezilla dig. We'll talk about *that* later." She winks, wiggles her fingers at me, and strolls away.

I'm still shaking my head at her goofy antics when my phone chimes next to me. A quick glance at the screen has my pulse accelerating as the buzz in my stomach.

> *Rowen: Sweetheart?*

I scroll up to discover there are a few missed messages from earlier.

> *Rowen: We just landed and I'm already counting the minutes until we leave again.*

> *Rowen: How many cups of coffee so far?*

> *Rowen: I'm going to assume it's a busy morning at work and*

you're not dodging me on purpose. I miss you, Vix.

How did I not see these?

Instant guilt and worry attack my renewed determination as the familiar destruction comes barging in.

Will he forget about me now?

Does he think I'm too busy for him?

I chop down those shitty thoughts before they take root. Rowen is different and I won't ruin this by letting the real crazy get ahold of me. I can't stop my hands from trembling but my response gets sent regardless.

> Me: *I'm glad you arrived safely. Sorry it took a bit to respond. I didn't hear my phone. Willow was in here.*

Of course he responds instantly—crushing any lingering doubt.

> Rowen: *There's my girl. Thought you ran off on me and I'd have to chase you all over again.*

Seriously, this man is what dreams are made from. Not sure I'll ever tell him that but . . .

> Me: *Still here, Casper. I'm not planning on ditching you anytime soon.*

I'm giving in. The pounding in my soul won't stop until I try. Rowen would be the only one, the perfect match for me. He'd be the end, my prince in the castle. If I let the walls crumble and obliterate my defense shields, he can be all mine. I'll be completely exposed and vulnerable—no more hiding and running away scared. I'm about to dive in, cannonball splash style, with my entire body.

Am I ready for that?

Hell yes.

FOURTEEN

Rowen

'm hauling ass over to Xander's house since the party started almost an hour ago. Being late makes my blood pressure rise, especially when people are waiting on me. I was supposed to pick up Lark on the way but couldn't at the last minute, which adds another pound of tension already locking up my muscles.

Remaining stress from the flight delay still lingers but soon enough Lark will be in my arms. Then I'll chill the hell out after being trapped in the air way too long. When the plane's wheels finally touched down on Minnesota soil, solid relief revved through me like I've never felt before—not even when I first returned from deployment and that's really saying something.

It's so fucking good to be home.

Almost two weeks away was tough as shit, but hopefully worth the hassle. We ended up extended our trip our week, which was unexpected but necessary. Lincoln has a buddy from his army days that contacted us about setting up a potential partnership. The brothers you serve with are family forever even after getting out and moving on. Apparently Brock Kason has found a ton of success after being discharged and wants to share the wealth.

Now he's some hot-shot exec for the fancy investment agency we toured and his company is planning to open a branch in Minneapolis. Seems like they're in need of guard detail and we're just the guys for the job.

Brock's account will provide an enormous payday and is the big break we've been hoping for. The possibility of Sworr Security expanding sooner rather than later is looking real solid. This huge boost has me believing luck is on my side. I just have to lock down my girl and everything will be aces.

My tires screech as I slam on the brakes after roaring into the driveway. I practically sprint to the backyard, searching for Lark with longing clawing at my skin. My anxious gaze finds her immediately, like a heat-seeking missile locking onto its target. As my eyes devour the sight of her slender figure hidden by flowing fabric, the royal blue material billows around her and looks like ocean waves. I'm stunned motionless by Lark's angelic beauty. The air whooshes from my lungs after holding it too long.

I'm such a lucky bastard.

She's perfection personified and completely mine, whether we've slapped a label on our relationship or not. I'm ready to seal the deal and make us official so she better be prepared. I'm done goofing around with the flirty texting bullshit that's occupied our time for the last fourteen days.

I sneak up behind Lark and wrap my arms around her thin waist. Her intoxicating vanilla scent infiltrates my senses and instantly calms my racing pulse. I lean in close and softly kiss her delectable neck. She tenses momentarily until I whisper, "I've missed you, Sweetheart."

Lark sags against me as she tucks her face into mine. "I was wondering if you'd ever show up, Casper." Her breath fans along my cheek. "I might have missed you too." Those simple words fill me with scorching heat and the sudden urge to get her alone overtakes me.

"Let me make it up to you." I murmur quietly in her ear.

"What did you have in mind?" Her breathy voice reflects desire.

"Several things, *so many things*, but first we need to get away from this crowd. I'm not interested in putting on a show."

Lark trembles slightly before a tiny moan escapes her tempting mouth. Her hand reaches up to grip my shirt to pull me even closer. Her red-stained lips brush against my jaw as she seductively blows out a puff of air. My entire body shakes from the seemingly small act since I've been depriving myself for years. Lark's gentle movements send a scalding blast straight to my dick.

A ragged swallow traps the groan climbing up my throat but the desperate sound tumbles out after she hums, "Yes."

That one syllable sets me in motion and the only thing that matters is getting Lark somewhere private. When I glance up to check our surroundings and find the fastest exit, Willow and Xander are staring at us. The happy couple have differing expressions covering their features, from shock to smug awareness, but now isn't the time to analyze their faces. We'll catch up later.

Losing control.

Bursting.

Arousal pumps through my veins in a wild rhythm and control is quickly slipping from my grasp. I want her.

Bad.

It's time to claim what's always belonged to me.

"Let's go," is forced out between clenched teeth while I attempt to keep my cock under control. I refuse to bust in my pants with everyone watching. Without pausing for her response, I start stumbling carelessly backwards to drag Lark inside the house. She's shielding the party guests from my obvious erection and I don't mind being pressed against her luscious ass one bit. Our clumsy steps jerk the connection between us and blows my fucking mind.

Once we're through the screen door, I wildly scan the empty

space for a room we can occupy. Lark wiggles in my hold but she's not going anywhere.

She breaks the silence. "If you'd let me turn around, I can show you where the bathroom is. Down the first hallway on the right."

My uncontrollable desire has taken over and everything around me is covered with a lusty haze. I notice the room she's referring to and quickly move us in that direction. There's no stopping to switch positions, even though walking backward isn't the quickest or smoothest. We almost topple over while crossing the threshold but manage to stay upright. I spin Lark around to face me and can't decide what to do first. My frantic thoughts are scattered with endless possibilities. I clench my eyes shut before taking a deep inhale—trying to get a fucking grip—but the effort evaporates as my sight devours her again.

In the next moment, we're locked in the bathroom and Lark's back is shoved against the closed door. Her chest rapidly rises and falls with panting breaths while her fingers reach for me. The silver arrow resting along her collarbone is like a brand—*mine*. Her amber orbs are glowing with want—*for me*. I haven't even touched her and my dick throbs with the threat of exploding. My starving stare feasts on each visible piece of flesh, which isn't much, considering her outfit choice.

"You always wear short dresses. Every time I've seen you, except today. Why did you wear a long skirt? What am I supposed to do with all that extra stuff?" My hands motion to the offensive fabric I'm referring to.

Without answering, Lark swings her leg out to the side. The change in stance exposes a high slit that was previously hidden. I rumble loudly at the goddess spread out before me. This woman is trying to kill me.

"*Fuck*. It's like a trapdoor, just for me. My sexy little Vixen," I mumble softly while stepping into her body.

Her voice is a purr, luring me even closer. "You like it, Casper?"

Is she blind?

My cock is so hard the zipper is about to rip off the seams. I rub my hard length against her softness.

"Yeah, Sweetheart. You've got me so worked up, one stroke is all it will take." Sounds ridiculous but I'm not exaggerating. My lack of physical contact mixed with her overt hotness is a recipe for me coming embarrassingly fast.

A throaty laugh bubbles from her and the sound sends another direct hit to my groin. Lark digs her fingers into my hips before sliding her palms around to my ass. She draws me in tighter before rocking her core along my straining cock. Her back arches, pushing her tits against my chest, before she stretches forward to reach my ear.

"Now that you have me here, what will you do with me?" Her suggestion is clear but this will only be an introduction for what I have planned. Lark hasn't told me everything I want to hear about our future but she will, especially after I get my tongue on her.

My hand snakes up her bare thigh as my mouth lowers to hers. "Vix, are you wet for me?"

She sucks in a sharp breath before nodding quickly. Lark tips her chin up, our lips almost touching. I drop a peck to her ruby pout as a short tease while my palm continues up her satin skin.

When I reach the apex of her thighs and meet naked flesh, my balls tighten with an irresistible urge to blow but I bite my tongue to stave off the release.

What the actual fuck is this little vixen trying to do?

Choking out my reaction is a challenge. "No panties, Vix? You're so fucking naughty and I love it." I nip her jaw before licking away the sting. She tastes like vanilla frosting and I want to devour every delicious inch.

My fingers glide through her wetness and Lark moans against my mouth. "Fuck, Rowen. That feels so fantastic. Don't stop."

"Are you aching, Sweetheart? Do you need me?" My thumb

finds her clit before circling around the tiny bundle.

"Yes. *Please.*" Her plea echoes around the room.

My mouth slams down onto hers and she eagerly opens as our lips seal and tongues collide. The smooth slide compliments the sensual rhythm of my fingers' ministrations. Lark begins to quiver, her arms trembling around me as her knees almost buckle. I press harder into her, *everywhere*, before putting a bit of space between us. Lark tries following me as my face eases away so I dive back for another searing kiss.

I nibble along her bottom lip while stroking my knuckles through her slit. We're both gasping when I pull away and start sucking down her neck to her collarbone. As I begin lowering myself down, Lark seems to snap out of her breathless trance.

"What are you doing?" A hint of panic slips into her voice.

"I need to taste you, Sweetheart. I want to feel you explode on my tongue." My words are muffled against her stomach as I settle onto my knees.

Lark tries to yank me back up and the similarities to that disastrous encounter at her apartment a few weeks ago don't escape me. Her fingers scratching along my scalp shoot sparks down my spine and encourage me to continue my quest. I begin gathering the excess material of her skirt and pushing it to the side when Lark starts struggling.

My gaze is hazy as I glance up at her. "Sweetheart, what's wrong?"

"You don't need to do that. Really. Just keep touching me like before."

"But I want to, Vix. I need every piece of you. Why won't you let me?"

"It's not necessary. I probably won't even like it." Her tone goes soft and hesitant as her gaze darts off to the side.

"The fuck? What do you mean? You've never had a man go down on you before?"

Lark scoffs. "Why would I? Guys don't like doing that so it's no big deal." She sighs loudly before adding, "Maybe we should just go back outside." For her it's better to avoid the situation, but not anymore. Not with me.

"I'm not sure what morons you've dated but that's a crock of shit, Vix. I enjoy eating pussy and I'm going to *love* feasting on yours. Just relax and tell me what feels good, okay?" I try to keep the frustration from my voice after imagining Lark with those selfish idiots. She's mine now and each part of her deserves to be spoiled, which definitely includes her satin center.

Her timid nod is all it takes. Without further delay, I effortlessly hitch her leg over my shoulder to spread her wide open for me. She wobbles slightly before gripping onto me harder for balance. Her touch ignites a blaze of burning thirst so intense it makes me fucking light-headed.

"I love your hands on me, Vix. Dig those nails in and leave your mark." The order is rushed as my face dips toward her bare core.

My nose rubs through her damp sex while inhaling the naturally sweet aroma. I suck and nip her glistening lower lips before flattening my tongue to lap up her essence. She tastes so fucking good, I want to savor every drop before digging in again.

"*Holy shit!* What are you doing to me, Rowen? That . . . oh God, yes!" Lark's incoherent sounds spur me on and I start really going after her.

My mouth latches onto her clit while my finger eases into her, pumping shallowly through her tight walls. One of her hands slides through my hair before grasping the thick strands, pulling almost painfully at my roots. I attack her pulsing button with rapid flicks before swiveling a figure-eight pattern against the sensitive nerves.

Lark's entire body shudders as she mewls out more garbled nonsense. Her noises encourage me to work harder as she begins to convulse around me.

My cock is weeping with pre-cum and listening to Lark's seductive cries isn't helping. I'd rather not make a mess in my shorts so with a sly flick of my wrist and a few stealthy maneuvers, I get the button open and the zipper lowered. I moan as the cool air wraps around my heated flesh. The vibrations from my throat has Lark shrieking and clawing at my scalp. I groan louder while lapping faster at her pussy.

Her trembling form bows away from the wall as her orgasm takes over. My sunken digit is sucked deeper into her fluttering core and her honey pools on my tongue. Without warning, fierce pleasure radiates from my balls and shoots warmth through my cock. I'm floating on an erotic high as tingling sparks rapidly spread out from my groin. My own climax plows into me but I don't stop my wild attack on Lark's body.

Her muscles are tightly locked around me with passionate tension as she continues riding her release. My jaw aches as I slowly withdraw from her heat, which is already tempting me back for more. While Lark is still swirling in a blissful state, I find some tissue to clean up the floor. No one wants to see that shit.

Her breathing begins to calm as I stand and tuck in my junk. Lark's amber irises gleam with relief as her relaxed figure sags against the door. The goofy grin lifting her lips makes me chuckle because she's cute as hell, ruined and wrecked after I showed her how amazing it can be.

When Lark is finally able to collect her thoughts, her voice is scratchy.

"Jesus, *that's* what I've been missing? Where the hell have you been all my life and when can we do that again?" Awareness seems to flicker in her caramel eyes before she asks, "Wait, what about you?"

She blew my fucking mind without even touching my dick. "Don't worry about me, I got off just fine. And we can have a repeat performance soon enough, Sweetheart. Can you take a few days off work?"

Lark furrows her brow while glancing down at my pelvic region—currently lacking the typical erection I'm sporting whenever she's around. If she keeps looking at me that way, the reprieve will wear off before I'm even halfway down.

The confusion clouding her features clears a bit as my question registers. "What? Why?"

"It's a surprise but I'm planning something special. Just say yes."

"If you'll give me more of that," she gestures to my mouth, "absolutely. When can we leave?"

FIFTEEN

Lark

"Do you think Xander and Willow know we christened their bathroom?" Rowen asks with a smirk on his face.

"Trust me, those walls have seen far worse." I laugh at his slack-jaw expression. "Do you know our friends at all? They can't keep their hands off each other for a minute."

"I guess. Thanks for pointing it out. Now I have the vision Xander's naked ass burned into my brain." He retorts with that same horrified look covering his features.

"Why are you picturing him? Or maybe I don't want to know . . ." I let my silly suggestion hang in the air between us. Messing with Rowen is too fun.

His head whips my way while still keeping an eye on the road. "Real funny, Vix. So, you'd rather have me imagine your friend?"

I point at him accusingly but keep the humor in my tone. "Don't start with me, Casper. We are so not swinging with them."

Rowen brings our clasped hands to his lips and kisses my wrist. The feel of his mouth on my skin shoots off a thousand sparklers all over me. "Sweetheart, you're the only one for me.

Pretty sure we've been over that." He murmurs along my palm.

There's my cue to melt into a warm puddle of love-goo. If Rowen keeps talking like this, we'll never make it to wherever it is he's taking me. We've already been in the truck for almost eight hours and I'm getting antsy as hell. Our conversations have been pretty tame so far but maybe he's ready to get more . . . intimate.

"I suppose you've mentioned your feelings a time or two but we haven't really talked about it. Tell me what you want, Rowen." The words ooze out while I lean toward him and glide my fingers up his arm.

"Vix, there is plenty I want but we'll be speaking face to face when you hear it. I'm not pouring my soul out while driving."

I huff and sit back in mock-frustration. "How much longer?"

He snickers before belting out a sharp hoot at my pout and raised brow. "You're adorable, and almost too sexy for me to resist, but this is important to me. We're about thirty minutes out."

"And where are we going exactly?" I've asked this before and he won't budge so curiosity has been tickling at me this entire time. It's really difficult to sit still for this long without knowing what lies ahead.

And I'm more than ready to find out.

He hums softly before sending me a grin that releases the swoony flutters inside me—*sigh*. Then he whispers, "You'll see, Sweetheart."

Rowen wasn't joking around about his plans. Once I agreed last night—while euphoria was thrumming through my veins—he wanted to leave immediately but we couldn't ditch the party. After I explained how important the festivities were to Willow, and by extension Xander, Rowen relented and agreed we would take off in the morning.

The evening was better than a typical bachelorette bash because honoring the pair together was more special. Pretty sure Rowen didn't mind walking around their yard, holding my hand,

and practically shouting that we are couple. I couldn't stop myself from picturing us in their place but I kept thinking it's way too soon for that.

I glance over at him, wearing his aviator shades and a delicious amount of stubble, and now think maybe not. A pinch of panic hits me with those thoughts because I already love him and it terrifies me. I'm handing over my heart and Rowen better take damn good care of it.

Time passes quickly as I get lost in daydreams of a white gown, a certain someone at the end of the aisle, and exchanging vows of forever. We veer down a heavily wooded path before an enormous cabin comes into view and my breath catches at the sight before me. The gorgeous building is made up of natural brown wood, colorful stone, and huge windows. It extends so far and wide that portions are hidden from view but I can't wait to explore every square foot.

Rowen busts out laughing suddenly and I'm sure it's because my mouth is hanging open in shock. It's a struggle to peel my eyes away from the stunning rustic mansion but I manage. The view of his handsome face lit up with delight is even better than our vacation spot and a weighty exhale leaves me as I get lost in his genuine smile.

"What you do think, Vix? Can you handle spending a few days here?" Rowen's excited tone reflects the joy on his features and I can't help but stare in wonder.

I am totally gone for this man.

He squeezes my hand before asking, "Sweetheart? You alright?"

All I manage is a jerky nod and a long hum of approval. He chuckles again and seems to understand that's the extent of my communication abilities at the moment. Rowen swoops in for a quick kiss on my gaping lips before telling me to get moving.

"Let's go check the place out. Get in there while I grab the bags. The key should be under the mat." He commands as he begins gathering our stuff from the backseat. I don't need to be told twice.

Scampering out of the truck, I take a few minutes to appreciate the outdoor scenery. There are beautifully blooming flowers spread over the landscaping and the color combinations create a vibrant rainbow over the ground. The cabin has a massive wraparound porch that makes me bubble with glee as I picture sitting out here with Rowen while watching the sunrise. Of course there are two perfectly placed rocking chairs specifically for that reason. This is definitely a spot where magic is meant to happen.

After finding the key and letting myself in, I visually inhale the vast array of countrified details displayed throughout house. Every piece of décor has a place and it heightens the overall allure that much more. The entire back wall facing the river is mainly glass and I'm completely mesmerized when I lay eyes on the captivating view. That's how Rowen finds me.

He envelops me in a warm embrace that has me envisioning a fantasy future once again. Right here, in this majestic space with his capable arms holding me tight, it's ridiculously easy to imagine. Tears blur my vision at the fairytale laid out in front of me, so close I can practically feel the warm glow of a happily ever after. The promising potential blankets me with soft velvet as my heart finds true love—*finally*.

Could this be my life? For real?

"Really something, right?" Rowen whispers in my ear.

I shiver slightly from his heated breath before uttering, "It's so wonderful." My words echo the faraway enchantment I'm absorbed in and soothing swirls are floating through me. It's almost like an out-of-body experience and I never want to wake up.

Rowen gently kisses my shoulder and asks, "Do you want to take a walk?"

His question pulls me from my stupor but I'm feeling a tad

foggy from the lingering bliss. Spotting a fire pit nestled in the yard makes me hungry for s'mores. "Can we have a fire instead? Then take a walk tomorrow? It's almost dark anyway."

"That sounds nice, Sweetheart. We can get all hot and bothered by the flames before I really heat you up." His voice is practically a growl as he nibbles along my neck.

"Maybe we skip the fire and explore the bedroom instead." I'm already wet and practically panting in his embrace. The romantic setting mixed with his seductive tone is the best foreplay. This will be a long-ass night if we're going to tease each other with what's to come.

A low groan rumbles from his chest. "Vix, you're killing me with those squirming thighs and swaying hips. Are you aching for me again?" Rowen leans in to nip at my jaw before sucking the tender skin. He's stirring up a crazy amount of want within me.

After licking a slow path up my throat, he rests his chin on top of my head. "But let's wait a bit longer, Sweetheart. It will be more fun to drag it out. Plus, you've been so eager for me to tell you what I want. Tonight I'll tell you *everything*." The way Rowen emphasizes that word has quivers erupting in my core. I turn around to face him and gaze deeply into his sapphire stare.

"*Yes.*" The plea is desperate as he continues alternating bites and licks against my sensitive skin. But then Rowen decides *no.* He abruptly pulls away and I want to scream in frustration. This guy has serious willpower.

I reach up and palm his scruffy cheek. "You better, Casper. I can hardly wait."

Rowen releases me from his hold but snags my hand before leading us out a side door.

"Do you own this place?" I ask.

"I wish. It belongs to an army buddy of mine. We came out here a few times for R&R. I figured you'd love it. He gladly agreed to let us borrow it when I asked." He explains while getting the fire going. The wood starts burning immediately and I'm not at all surprised by his outdoorsy skills.

I sit in an empty chair and bask in the heat already rising around us. "It's very serene and peaceful. I definitely understand why you escaped out here to relax."

There's nothing around other than trees and the whisper of the flowing river. Although a gravel path appears to cut through the forest along the right side so maybe it leads to another house. I try peering deeper into the woods from my seat but can't see much beyond the winding driveway. Before I can ask, Rowen spins and stalks forward before effortlessly scooping me up. Then he takes a seat with me straddling his lap.

It all happens so quickly I'm a bit woozy but his whispered confession steadies me. "Pretty sure this is the ultimate spot to fall madly in love, too."

He closes the sliver of space between our mouths until we're breathing each other in. This kiss is different than any other we've shared. It's a slow, languid slide of lips and tongues. There's no reason to rush and our bodies are taking proper time to explore each other. This mellow connection silently speaks of devotion and affection. I practically merge into him as scorching shivers take over. He must feel the pleasurable tremble in my limbs because the subdued tempo suddenly snaps.

His muscular arm ropes around my back before yanking me closer until I feel Rowen's undeniable hardness between my legs. His other hand roams up my shirt and his rough palm meets the smooth skin on my side. I glide my fingers up his chest and shoulders before weaving them into his thick hair. He moans as my nails scratch along his scalp and the vibration is electrifying.

I rock into him as my head tilts to deepen the kiss. Rowen takes advantage of the new angle and begins feasting on my mouth. His tongue strokes along mine as he sucks my lips between his teeth. He thrusts up so his rigid length rubs along my seam just right. It's my turn to whimper as more intense shocks pulse from my core.

The intrusive crunch of gravel puts an abrupt halt on our steamy make-out session as our heads simultaneously whip toward the sound. Bright headlights stun my straining eyes and white spots dance around while my vision adjusts. Rowen's truck is big but the approaching vehicle is effing enormous—the tires alone are taller than me. I chuckle that the owner might be compensating for something.

A man and woman are illuminated by the flames as they slowly drive by so I offer a welcoming wave. "Are those the neighbors?" I ask while turning back to Rowen. "I saw a path over there earlier and wanted to ask if anyone lived nearby. Hopefully they weren't scandalized by our smooching."

His nose brushes along mine as he whispers against my lips. "I don't know who the hell they are other than an interruption. Although it's a good thing they showed up so I didn't strip you naked out here for anyone else to see." His hungry growl is back and the prickles sprinting along my skin has become an instinctual response.

Rowen licks along my neck before groaning loudly. "You taste so fucking delicious, Vix. I can't wait until my mouth is between your delectable thighs again." His naughty words have my cheeks heating in a mixture of excitement and anxiety. I'm still unsure about him going down on me but he really seems to enjoy it.

Before I can respond, snapping twigs and stumbling footsteps echo in the dark. An extremely attractive couple enters our little clearing and my earlier assumption is immediately proved false. The man is seriously massive and no doubt needs a truck that size to accommodate his enormous frame. The girl is gorgeous and looks far too polished for being out here in the woods.

Before my gawking gets awkward, I break the silence. "Hey! You guys are more than welcome to join us." Suddenly realizing

I'm still firmly planted on Rowen's lap, I scooch out of his arms and plop down in an empty spot.

The woman smirks at my not-so-stealthy move before saying, "I'm Brittany and this is my boyfriend Nathan. I hope you don't mind us coming down to say hello."

"I'm Lark and this is my . . ." My voice trails off as I glance at Rowen. We really need to chat about what's going on between us.

Of course he jumps to my rescue. "Her boyfriend, Rowen. Nice to meet you both." We all take turns exchanging the obligatory nods and handshakes.

Once they've sat down across from us, Brittany tilts her head slightly with curiosity. Her light blue eyes shine brightly. "Where are y'all from?"

"We're from Minnesota. Came down here to get away for a bit and relax. Figured this scene wouldn't hurt while I'm trying to really make it official with Lark." Rowen pipes up with far too much information.

My cheeks burn as I say, "Rowen! Seriously? They don't need to know all that." I roll my eyes with extra exaggeration. "Sorry about him. Where are you guys from?"

Nathan and Brittany exchange a knowing look before sharing a laugh. "We're from Arkansas. Let's just say we've been dealing with a lot lately and needed to get away also." She explains while warming her palms with the crackling fire. I've always loved a southern accent and Brittany's twang is extra sassy. I'm a huge fan.

We sit and chat comfortably while time whittles away. They seem to have their fair share of trouble in the recent past, which reminds me a lot of our rocky journey. All too soon, Brittany and Nathan need to get back to their sleeping son. I hug her because, well, she seems like a distant bestie, and send him off with a casual wave. Pretty sure my arms wouldn't reach around his bulky form if I tried.

When Rowen and I are alone, we hover in taut stillness while waiting for the other to make a move. Our heated gaze is locked and loaded, ready to explode with desire. He's the first to crack.

"Sweetheart, you don't want to be my girlfriend?" His hushed words appear to yell through the empty space separating us. His eyes shine in the firelight and seem to be pulling me closer.

I shake my head slightly, lost in his soulful stare. "Of course I do, Casper. I just didn't want to assume. And in my defense, we haven't discussed all that yet."

Rowen hums before sucking his plump lower lip between his teeth, which causes me to fidget restlessly on the chair. "We're so far past the point of assuming anything. I want you. Always. Just believe in us and you'll always be right."

Now my head is bobbing in acceptance as I whisper, "Okay. I'm very happy you're my boyfriend." I send him a playful smirk and the blinding smile he gives me in return stalls my heart. We hold each other captive in a dreamy gaze, saying so much without uttering another word. Rowen breaks after my tongue peeks out at him in suggestion.

"Should we go inside?"

"I thought you'd never ask." My words are barely audible as Rowen stands and looms over me. My pussy clenches uncontrollably at his visible bulge that's front and center. Without warning, I'm once again whisked into his grasp before we're hustling back to the cabin.

My stare is focused on Rowen's bobbing throat as he strides down what I assume is the hallway. "Are you nervous, Casper?" I whisper against his stubbled skin.

He draws me closer into his chest before muttering, "Fuck yes." Another heavy swallow. "My plan is to pour everything out, have you reciprocate, and make dirty love to you all fucking night. Seeing as I'm about to proclaim some serious stuff, not to mention going three years without sex, I'm a tad edgy."

"Are you sure I'm worth it? You've waited so long." I can't

help insecurity from seeping out.

"Sweetheart, I wasn't waiting. All this time, I was searching for you." Rowen sweetly murmurs, knowing exactly what I need to hear. He lays me on a billowy bed, the puffy comforter extra soft against my sizzling skin, before settling in next to me. Propping himself up on an elbow, Rowen stares deeply into my eyes while sweeping stray strands of blonde away from my face. The way he's looking at me causes my insides to go haywire with a mixture of desperate longing, skittering nerves, and twirling adoration. I'm completely head-over-heels and ready to finally admit the truth.

Rowen places a barely-there peck against my lips that has me soaring. But when he starts talking, I'm effing done for. "You're about to get everything from me, Sweetheart. I hope you're on the same page." I attempt to assure him because there isn't a sliver of doubt, but he covers my mouth with his and stops my admission. His soft touch is gone before I can plead for more but Rowen is just getting started. "I'm glad you're so eager to tell me whatever it is you have to say but let me get this off my chest first."

I lean into him until we're kissing but it's brief and innocent. Mostly because the gentle caress feels exquisite but it's also a sign for him to continue with confidence because I'm along for the ride.

"Go ahead, Casper."

"Have I told you how much that outrageous nickname means to me?"

"Does this have anything to do with the speech you've prepared?"

"Nah. I just wanted to let you know. The fact you took time to think of something to call me, no matter how silly, was a sure sign this would eventually work out."

The giggle flies out before I can trap it. "Oh yeah? Well, it started as a taunt but if I'm being honest, it's pretty cute. Now get to the good stuff. Tell me what you want already." The fake impatience in my voice causes a stunning smile to light him up.

My vision bounces around his happy features, ready to hear the words he's created just for me. Rowen's joyful snicker shakes my entire body since we're pressed so close. With laughter still painting his tone, he busts out the words every girl is desperate to hear.

"I love you so much, Sweetheart."

SIXTEEN

Rowen

That wasn't exactly how I expected this epic reveal to start but I couldn't hold back. Her eyes are shimmering like golden ambers and reflect pure happiness and humor. One minute she's cracking me up and the next, I'm blatantly turned on.

I devour the sight of her spread out along side of me, golden locks blanketing the pillow while she relaxes comfortably in my embrace. My blurted confession will be the only thing that happens prematurely tonight though. I hope Lark wasn't planning on getting much sleep while we're here.

But first, now that I've started . . .

"Pretty sure I've loved you since I stepped foot into Brack's Box seven years ago." A few beats pass while I pause for her reaction but my little vixen just silently stares at me, as if waiting for more.

"Is it my turn already? I figured there was more up your sleeve." Her snarky eyebrow is lifted as a smirk tilts her glossy lips.

"You're such a smartass, Vix. I'm trying to be romantic and you're stomping all over it." The amusement returns to my voice.

She scoffs with a wide-open mouth as a palm slaps her chest. "*Me?* You've been acting like there was some gigantic speech, but the sudden love reveal caught me off guard. You just threw it out there. Don't get me wrong, I'm really happy you feel that way because I do too." A hitch hits her voice. *"Oh my God,* I'm ruining this by being a bitch. Am I being a diva? What the hell is wrong with me? Rowen, I'm really sorry—"

"What did you say?" I cut off her ramblings as my mind snags on a few particular words.

"Which part? I'm being a bitch?"

"Nah, the feelings part."

Lark's caramel irises bore into me and pressure pounds in my ears. "I love you so much, Rowen. Of course I do." Her hand moves to cup my jaw so I lean down to seal her words with a kiss. I don't linger long—just a quick exchange of air through our slightly parted lips.

"I'm so fucking sorry about the past, Vix. If I didn't have to rush out that day, everything could have been different. We would have been together all this time. I should have been treasuring you in reality, not just my dreams. I'm not afraid to admit my obsession of a future with you. We could have been married with a family years ago." I huff, frustrated with fate or karma or whatever the hell kept us apart.

Her fingers keep rubbing along my jaw. "How do you know it would have worked out then? Maybe we were meant to be separated until now." Lark's response makes me wonder if she's a mind reader. She goes on before I can question her. "Sure it would have been nice to avoid the pain of rejection and heartache but who's to say it wouldn't have turned out even worse? Trust me, and I can't believe I'm saying this, but . . . Everything happens for a reason. Maybe I needed to be broken so you could piece me back together."

Fuck. This woman. She's my everything. And I can't wait until she's my wife.

"We should get married, Sweetheart."

"Easy there, tiger. No need to jump the gun. We just exchanged 'I love you', no need to fast forward to forever. I mean, we hardly know one another." She lets out an easy chuckle but her imploring eyes speak the truth her mouth won't admit. Lark is still worried this means more to her than me.

I smooth a finger down her flushed cheek before giving another huge part of me. "My mind doesn't have a collection of useless information stored up about you and my body hasn't felt your skin pressed against mine. But that's not what really matters since it's all surface level. What truly defines our connection goes so deep, we can't comprehend it. We can only give in. My heart beats a rhythm only you can understand. My soul lives for yours, united in a bond so strong nothing can break it. I don't know your favorite ice cream flavor or if you like butter on popcorn but in here," I tap my chest, "we have been together for eternity. Destiny brought us together. Our story has been written and we need to start reciting it." My breathing gets shallow after the words are out and my chest cramps with worry. Maybe that was too much, too far over the top. My anxious gaze frantically scans her features, seeking any sort of reaction.

When Lark's eyes mist and become glassy, it's like a punch to the gut. The air chokes out of me as panic threatens to clog my throat. But then she quietly asks, "Do you really mean it? Truly?" Worry and wonder saturate her tone.

My voice is still lost. All I can do is nod, my forehead resting against hers so the movement jostles both of us. Tears blur my own vision because the love pulsing between us is so fierce, it consumes every thought and demands to be recognized. I find the ink on her wrist before rubbing the decorated skin lightly.

When the emotion clears from my throat, I murmur softly against her jaw while continuing to stroke the tattoo. "Your heart isn't empty anymore. I want to fill it forever, with all my love. With everything I have to give."

I feel Lark swallow before taking a deep breath.

"All right. I'm impressed. You proved me wrong. *Again*. I'll stop questioning and just believe in you. In us." She sniffs lightly before chewing her bottom lip. "You're an amazing man and have a serious way with words. Pretty sure the jitters and butterflies are on constant assault." Another deep inhale. "I'm so effing grateful you're all mine."

Even in the serious moments, she makes me laugh. *"Damn."* I sigh against her adorable pout. "I love you so fucking much. This," I gesture down my body, "is definitely all yours, Vix."

Lark's tongue peeks out between her teeth, looking like a naughty tease. "Are you ready to show me now?" Her palm drags across my pecs and abs before playing with the waistband of my shorts.

"My words aren't enough, huh?" Lark's feisty side lights me up and I eagerly play along.

Her fingers instantly disappear as her face crumples. "Of course that's enough. I wasn't trying to push you into anything. Let's just keep talking." She tries to pull away so I tighten the arm looped around her waist.

I snatch Lark's hand and return it to the button she'd been toying with. "I'm fucking around, Vix. I'm so hard my dick is about to explode."

She grips me, as if to test my honesty, before giggling. "How romantic."

"You wanted everything, right? You're about to get the fireworks show."

"Shall I *oooh* and *ahhh?*"

"Shut up and give me those sassy lips."

Lark doesn't hesitate and sags against me once our mouths meet. The snark from a moment ago evaporates as we get lost in our lust. She opens wider to accept more of my searching tongue. She sucks and strokes, giving me better than she's getting, as arousal rockets through me with ferocious intensity. It doesn't take long before I'm rolling on top of her while diving deeper into our connection. Lark is pushed into the mattress as my weight covers her entire body—my hulking form swallowing up her petite figure. Her nails are scratching into my back through the cotton t-shirt but I want to feel her dig into my skin.

Easing onto an elbow, I grip the collar and yank the fabric over my head. Then I'm back at her lips, frantically devouring her while she moans into my mouth. Lark arches up so her covered tits push against my naked flesh. Her fingers are digging into my ass while my hands are threaded through her silky flaxen locks. I'm licking while she's lapping and it feels like a sexy battle of tangled tongues.

Lark breaks away to pant in my ear, "I want you, Rowen. *Now.*" Her hips bump up, as if encouraging me, so I grind my solid cock along her center.

"Sweetheart, you're going to get it. But first I need to taste you again." My deprived dick will bust in two thrusts so I'll make damn sure she gets off first.

She's shaking her head violently against me. "No, I don't want that now. I need to feel you inside of me. *Please*, Rowen. Don't make me wait anymore." Lark's voice trembles while she tries pulling my shorts down.

I hum happily at her attempts and rock into her. "My girl is eager and that really turns me on." I growl against her neck before nipping the soft skin. "You won't let me go down on you?"

"Later, if you really want. Now get naked. I want to see all of you." Her thighs shift and shake a bit while she murmurs urgently. The urge to argue further pings around my brain for a beat before I realize she's practically begging me to fuck her, and I'm making her wait.

I suck and lick along her throat, dragging my tongue down until I reach the low-rise neckline of her shirt. My teeth softly bite into the top of her tits where the pillowy flesh is shoved up from her bra. I moan and add more suction when Lark suddenly bucks her pelvis.

"You're driving me crazy, Rowen. I'm fucking burning up for you. Hurry up and unleash that giant from your pants."

My chuckle vibrates off her cleavage before I push up to my knees. "I'm trying to take my time and make this good for you, Sweetheart. Why do we need to rush?" My heated gaze eats up her writhing body as my rough palms begin sliding up her torso, removing the obstructive clothing as I go.

Lark bows to make my task easier while gliding up my forearms with her hungry hands. "Because I can't stand it anymore. My heart and soul crave you, Casper. I need to be one with you."

Her words hit me square in the chest and I'm sure she feels the shudder rattle through me. "Fuck, Sweetheart. That sounds real good coming from your sweet mouth. I love you, Vix."

Once her shirt is off, her glowing ambers seer into me again. "I love you too, Rowen." Those words tunnel into me and suddenly a desperate ache to bury myself in her pussy takes over.

My fingers find the clasp of Lark's bra while she works on taking off my shorts. After those get stripped off, the only barrier separating us are my briefs and her panties. My already throbbing cock practically jerks at the obvious wetness from her core. The silk is drenched and her desire threatens to dissolve any remaining control I have left.

I'm still distracted by the sight in front of me when Lark begins lowering my boxers. Her gasp has my chest clenching in concern, until her fingers wrap around my dick. "You've kept this beautiful piece locked away for three years? That's an injustice to women and the human race. You should be showing off this bad boy to everyone. Look at how perfect he is." She's cooing at my fucking penis like he's her new favorite toy, which wouldn't be the worst thing.

Ready to show her what all that waiting has done, I rip the scanty cloth from between her legs before kicking off my briefs. I grab her thighs and spread them wider while fitting into the juncture. Lark loops her legs around me and draws me in, which has my cock pressed tight to her hot pussy. My stomach presses against her belly as I lower myself down.

My mouth is hungry when I latch onto hers, tongues thrashing as our hips begin flexing together. I slip through her slick slit, setting a rolling rhythm. Lark's throaty moans ignite passion in my veins and the friction against my dick has me seeing stars.

"Tell me you're mine." My demand is murmured against her swollen lips.

"I'm yours."

My palm roams from her ass up along her quivering side. "Always?"

"Yes."

"Forever?" I question while my fingers gently pinch her nipple and twist slightly.

Lark gasps, "And ever."

"You'll be my wife?"

"When you ask me right."

"*Mmmm*." I buzz along her jawline.

That sounds damn good to me.

The wait is over as I adjust until my tip nudges at her scorching entrance. As I'm sinking into her, my skin is hypersensitive and each millimeter feels like a mile. I push in slowly, almost painfully so, while Lark's cries get louder and more insistent. She wants me *deeper* and *faster* and *harder* but all I can focus on is the tight clamp her pussy has on me. Lark stretches and welcomes me further as my dick sighs in relief after so long without experiencing this sensation.

The farther I press in, the more forceful my urge to come gets, but I refuse to give in so soon. My jaw clenches as my eyes screw shut while I regain control and shove away from the brink. Everything seems heightened and electric as feverish sparks spread out from my groin. Nothing has ever felt so intense and I know it's because we're sharing more than our bodies—our souls are bonding as we become one.

I suck Lark's lip between my teeth and grunt when my cock fills her to the hilt. Being snugly wrapped in her depths causes my body to quake as I withdraw before slamming back in, much faster and harder this time. It's like muscle memory suddenly clicks and my rustiness evaporates with a manic thrust. Her smooth hands glide along my shoulders and slide into my hair while her back arches and her pelvis grinds against mine. She can't hold still and her frantic movements become more insistent as my pace increases. Each time I drive in, Lark screams and digs her claws into me. When I'm pulling out, her thighs cinch to keep me close.

My starving cock can't take much more before busting. "Wanna ride me, Sweetheart?"

"Hell yes."

We roll seamlessly and manage to remain locked together. Lark already looks thoroughly fucked as she straddles me with her bee-stung pout, messy tresses, and flushed chest. Her tits sway and bounce as she begins rocking against me, creating a tantalizing pattern by swiveling her hips and squeezing my dick tight as hell.

I plant my feet on the bed and pull my knees up so she can lean back against me. The angle gives me perfect access to her glistening clit and my thumb gets to work rubbing circles around the hard nub. My other hand palms her breast before clamping onto the stiff peak pointing right at me. Lark tosses her head back and releases a seductive scream. She's rambling about how I'm the best she's ever had and how amazing my big cock feels plowing into her.

That shit goes straight to my head, both of them, so I surge up and drive straight into her. She shrieks and slaps her palms onto my abs before following the ridges with her nails. The sting zips straight to my balls, which draw up even further. Lark's brown eyes are blasting me with golden flames while she continues gyrating at rapid speed.

I watch my cock disappear inside her while my knuckle keeps rounding her bundle of nerves. The erotic sight is snapping my control as the threat of release floods through me. I'm swelling impossibly larger as sparks rush up my spine.

"Rowen, I'm coming. Fuck, fuck! Yessss . . . don't stop. Holy shit, you're so fucking hard. *Oh my God!*" Her trembling body is a live wire as her core ripples around me.

I pinch her nipple hard while strumming her clit. My cock jerks as the climax washes over me and propels jets of cum into her clenching pussy. Our combined moans echo around the room and my ears ring from the sharp sounds. My muscles are tense and locked as extreme pleasure roars out within me. Lark keeps helplessly shuddering, begging and crying out.

Her figure goes limp and she collapses onto me. She's panting and twitching as apparent satisfaction blankets her. I'm dizzy as fuck and can't catch my breath but my exhausted limbs wind around my little vixen. My head rests against hers as my system reboots and begins regulating back to normal.

"Holy hell, Casper." Lark's rasp is straight sex and has me thinking about round two. She clears her throat. "Shit, you made my kitty purr real sweet. It's all throbby and tickly."

A hoarse chuckle rumbles up my throat. "You're so fucking hot, Vix. Even when you're talking nonsense." My fingers skim along her lower back before delving between her seam. "Want me to kiss her and make it even better?" I'm still desperate for her tangy taste.

"You didn't wear a condom so I'm probably a mess. Maybe after a shower, I'll lick you all up and blow your mind, too."

Her enticing suggestion almost makes me forget the lack of protection part. "Shit, Sweetheart. I forgot to wrap up. I'm such an ass." No wonder I could feel every smooth and soft curve.

"I'm on the pill so it's all good." She pauses and takes a deep breath. "You're the only one I've ever felt bare. I'm glad you didn't use anything."

"Fuck, Vix. I love that. *A lot*. Makes my possessive side very happy." I mumble against her hair before kissing her forehead. "Want to get clean so I can make you filthy again?"

"Only if you carry me. My legs feel like jelly."

SEVENTEEN

Lark

'm pressed up against the shower wall with Rowen's mouth between my thighs, one leg swung over his broad shoulder. It took all of thirty seconds under the spray before he dropped to his knees. The sweet romance has been stowed away and his naughty side is taking charge.

Another lazy lick drags up my slit and I shiver against the cool tile while water pelts against my heated skin. Any lingering hesitation about him doing this vanished after his first touch. There's no denying the extreme pleasure tingling from my clit and I never want it to stop.

Rowen kisses my mound before breaking away. "I need to hear you, Sweetheart. Last time I feasted on your delectable pussy we had to be quiet, but not this time. What do you want, Vix?" His smoky growl rumbles along my hip.

All I can do is whine and arch my pelvis forward, silently asking for more.

"Tell me, Sweetheart. Do you like this?" He asks while stroking a finger through my wetness.

"Yes," I murmur.

"What?"

"Yes!" The word rattles from my throat.

Rowen sucks along my lower belly and his question vibrates into me. "Want me to make you come?"

"Yes, please," I agree easily while nodding frantically.

"You're my dirty girl." His hooded blue gaze burns up at me. More wild head bobbing. "Uh huh. I am."

"Watch me eat you, Vix. I'm fucking starving and you need to see how much I enjoy this."

Rowen buries his face into my waiting pussy like he can't stay away another moment. My lids shutter rapidly as uncontrollable flutters take over when he laps along my seam. The pressure is already building as he finds my clit and latches on. A finger traces around my entrance in a teasingly slow pattern, driving my blistering need higher. My legs tremble while my feet twitch, like a reflex I can't control. I begin shamelessly rubbing harder against Rowen's mouth because the friction of his scruff along my sensitive skin is divine. I'm clutching handfuls of his luscious locks between my fingers and yanking him even closer. Rowen chuckles and the thrum shoots pulsing beats into me.

"More, more, more." The uncontrollable chant drops from my lips as my hips rock faster.

He hums and dives deeper, smashing his nose against my pubic bone while his tongue licks at my throbbing nerve bundle. My core is rippling gloriously as Rowen's fingers plunge in and discover my g-spot.

Holy fuck.

I'm boiling and whirling and melting while his assault on my pussy continues. My release is looming right in front of me as my pelvis swivels with Rowen's rhythm. As I climb higher and higher, my insides liquefy and begin to bubble. Molten lava fills my veins and blinding sparks race up my back when he nips my clit before sucking even harder. Heat emanates from my core and floods my system with a type of pleasure I've never experienced. The trembling in my limbs can't be controlled and I don't care to try as my gyrating figure slides against the slick wall.

My breathing is ragged as I pant out gobbledygook about how fucking amazing his mouth feels on me. His fingers spear and spread me wider, causing dark spots to dance in my vision. The desperation to come invades my brain until the need consumes me. Rowen is ruining me with this exquisite torture. His mouth is setting me ablaze and burning my body into a heap of smoldering embers so the gentle caress of his hands can resurrect me into something better, brighter, bolder. Without further warning, the orgasm to end all others rips into me viciously, and sends me soaring into the sky. Nonstop convulsions hijack my entire body while I float on a euphoric cloud.

When the earthquake within my core finally settles, I stare down into Rowen's roaring ocean stare and begin trembling for an entirely different reason. He's done the impossible by reconstructing my broken heart and I can't imagine my life without him. It no longer scares me. An uncontrollable desire to return the favor suddenly barrels into me and it has nothing to do with obligatory duty.

As Rowen breaks away from my thankful pussy and slowly rises, I take a moment to appreciate his hulking male beauty and impressive frame. He's made up of glowing golden flesh and perfectly sculpted muscles, but not the artificial shit you gain from a tanning booth or gym. Rowen's body is built from tough work and manual labor. A detailed American flag tattoo spans along his left side, starting near his hip and reaching toward his ribcage. My fingers had danced along the colorful lines when we'd been lying in bed but it was a brief graze. I was far too distracted prior to my current blissed-out state to appreciate the ink but the vision calls to me now. I'll have to ask more about it later.

Staring at Rowen gets me worked up all over again, especially when my eyes scan the length of his solid dick. His piece was created to give pleasure and I am happy to reap all the benefits, please and thank you. His cock is smooth steel encased in silky skin that I need to get my hands, and mouth, all over.

I eagerly reach for him. "Are you going to let me suck you off this time?" My words wheeze out while my palm strokes up his hardness.

Rowen's warm laugh distracts me from his dick momentarily while I glimpse up at him. Water sprays against his smiling face and I want to lick the droplets away. "What did I say about your smart mouth?"

"You love it?" I mutter against his wet jaw.

He groans and thrusts into my hand. "That I do and I'm sure it will look exquisite stretched around my dick."

Rowen's filthy words infuse me with confidence. This will be the best blowjob he's ever had and I'm making it my personal mission to have him coming in two minutes or less. Just because he makes me so fucking giddy. I place a searing kiss against his lips while pushing against him and turning until his back is along the wall. My mouth breaks away from his when I begin lowering myself.

I start with slow and deliberate licks around his crown, teasing his tip with what's to come. With long swirls, I lap at his cock like it's the most delicious ice cream treat. My hand wraps around his base but only my middle finger and thumb touch. I give him shallow pumps while moving my tongue further down his hardness. Rowen combs through my drenched hair before clutching my skull but he doesn't force my movements.

I've never been a huge fan of giving head. There isn't anything too appealing about shoving a stiff rod down your throat until you choke. But sucking Rowen's dick is so different; my mind is the one being blown. The silky texture glides along my tongue with every smooth pass. When I moan in delight, his knees practically buckle and that soaks my spirit with glee. His reaction encourages me to drag him in deeper and add stronger suction. Tears prick my eyes but I keep pushing. His cock brushes my tonsils and I relax to allow him in.

"Fuck, Sweetheart. I'm going to come already." Rowen moans when his entire length is in my mouth. "It's so fucking good, I don't think I can hold back. Your throat around me is the hottest fucking thing I've ever felt." His palm gently rests against my neck and I swallow so he feels it. "You're so fucking sexy, Vix." He purrs and stares down at me with heat so pure my legs tremble against the tile.

My teeth graze very lightly against his rigid flesh on the way out and expletives fly from Rowen's mouth. I fondle his tightening balls and silently cheer when his thighs clench. Using my tongue and lips to pull him back in, I suck extra hard and taste the start of his salty release. The hand still on my head tries to push me back but I remain latched around him.

"Sweetheart, I'm gonna blow." He warns but I just hum in response.

That's all it takes for him to explode deep in my mouth, an eruption of male flavor I eagerly take down. I milk Rowen dry and drink every drop.

"*Jesus Christ,*" he pants. "You suck cock like a naughty angel sent to pleasure only me and shit . . . that was fucking incredible."

My lips are still occupied as I buzz around his barely-softening cock. When my watery eyes glance up, I find Rowen's smoldering gaze burning holes into me. I giggle as I lick around his tip.

"Now you're in trouble, Vix." His sky-blue orbs gleam with mischief. "Making me bust down your throat like a fucking fire hose. We'll see who gets the last laugh." In the next breath, I'm tossed over his shoulder while he stalks out of the shower. There's no time for towels or drying off so we're leaving a trail of water, but that's not where my focus lies at the moment. Rowen's sexy ass is right in my face and I can almost stretch down to take a bite. I'm practically hypnotized by the sight as we bound down the hallway.

In the living room, Rowen sets me down and immediately bends me over the couch. In the next breath he plows into me from behind. A startled gasp escapes my lips before morphing into a passionate wail. My nipples tighten in pleasure as my pussy contracts from the sudden intrusion. He pins my arms down and the weighted pressure is fantastic. He rams into me with furious speed, our skin slapping with each aggressive thrust.

Rowen's knuckle brushes against my backside and I jolt forward, definitely not expecting the invasive touch. He chuckles darkly. "No?"

"That'd be a hell no, Casper." I snap over my shoulder, glaring at his filthy smirk.

He makes a noise I'm not too pleased with, as if he'll be changing my mind. "We'll see, Sweetheart." He leans down and whispers in my ear. "Remember I said everything." I shiver against him and know if he pushes the issue, I'll fold like a house of cards.

The subject gets dropped as Rowen's fingers pinch my clit before he resumes plunging into my pussy. I'll never get tired of feeling so full with him, and he makes sure I'm completely satisfied as we go at it for hours in numerous positions and on every available space.

In a corner chair, I climb on his lap backward and ride him until he lays us on the floor. He slides into me slowly on the bearskin rug before flipping me over and covering my body with his. After another round of epic orgasms, I suck him back deep into my throat while straddling his face as he tongues my slit.

Eventually we move off the ground and stumble along the cool hardwood as we prepare to dominate another space. Rowen hammers me into the kitchen wall before laying me across the counter with my legs around his waist. Then he bangs me against the staircase before fucking me in the entryway.

"Again?" Is his soft whisper between each climax and I'm always eager to agree.

"Yes. *Please, yes,*" I answer while spreading my legs wider or lifting my ass higher in invitation.

We make up for Rowen's three-year dry spell in one night and no area of the cabin is left untouched. Damn, I was one lucky ass recipient. He fucks and sucks me until my lady bits are weary and numb.

"I can't feel my vagina." I whine after we collapse into bed.

"Do you need me to revive her?" Rowen asks while dipping a few fingers into my exhausted pussy.

"*Oh, God.*" I moan while contemplating another round, but shove his hand away. "No more. I need rest you sex-fiend."

A hearty laughs bursts out of him. "I'm the nympho? Pretty sure I had you begging for more on multiple occasions."

I make a noncommittal sound. "Yeah, yeah. But now it's sleepy time."

And while the sun starts to rise over the river, we pass the eff out.

EIGHTEEN

Rowen

Waking up with Lark's naked body pressed against me is an experience I want every morning from now on. Her ass is cuddling with my dick, which has me harder than natural morning wood. I nuzzle into her neck before licking along the sensitive spot that drives her crazy. We went to bed a few hours ago so I should be taking advantage of sleeping in but there's much more appealing options.

I did filthy, unspeakable things to her last night and she fucking loved it. I already knew Lark was perfect before we had sex but damn, she exceeds that simple definition. It seems no matter what I toss her way, she responds with eager willingness and a few twists of her own. That blowjob? Fucking mind-melting. I've met my match in every possible way and we have the rest of our lives together.

With the light of a new day, the mood switch has been flipped back and it's time for softness again. I'm not a romantic in the slightest but this woman makes me want to be the biggest sap on the planet. For her, I'll do everything and anything she needs. Always.

My mouth keeps sucking on Lark's sweet vanilla skin until she stirs awake and arches further into me. That's all the invitation I need before slowly easing into her slick entrance. My little vixen was ready for me.

"Were you dreaming of me, Vix?" I murmur against her nape while gently rocking in and out. My palm roams up her side before cupping her luscious breast.

Lark's breath hitches before she moans. "You were doing exactly this. How did you know?"

I find her hand and intertwine our fingers before pulling her closer. "That's the way it works with soul mates, Sweetheart." Sentimental syrup keeps pumping through my veins and she seems to like my style. With more whispered words of endearment, we make sensual love until our bodies demand food.

After feeding each other breakfast, we get ready to explore the beautiful outdoors. I'd love to spend our getaway devouring Lark's body but we didn't trek all this way to stay trapped inside the cabin. My arm winds around her waist as I lead her through the backyard to the river.

"Can I ask you something, Casper?" Her breathy voice breaks the serene silence of the wilderness.

My heartrate skyrockets instantly because no good news ever starts with that question. I clear my throat while tightening my hold on her. "Let's hear it, Vix."

The expression on my face must show worry because Lark chuckles when she lifts her chin to look at me. "It's nothing bad, Rowen. I just want to know about your tattoo."

The breath I didn't realize was trapped in my lungs wheezes out in a relieved exhale. My ink isn't the easiest topic to discuss but I'll take it over her wanting to slow things down or some other bullshit. "I mentioned my fallen brothers before, right?" Lark nods slowly as I ease us to a stop before lifting up the hem of my shirt.

"So many lose their lives each day fighting for our country and this is a memorial for the soldiers in my troop. Their names and dates are scrawled within the white stripes of our flag." I explain while twisting my torso so she can see the men I'll never forget.

Her fingers dance along the permanent lines marking my skin while whispering, "There's so many. How tragic."

"War is fucking tragic, Vix." I inhale a sharp breath before continuing. "But they'll never be forgotten and they live on through all of us who made it out." My chest cramps in a painful knot as I remember my friends and sadness washes over me like it always does.

Fuck, I miss them all so much.

Lark's palm rests along my ribcage. "This is a lovely tribute, Rowen. You'll always have them close."

"Exactly," I murmur against her temple before kissing the soft skin.

"Can you tell me what you did in the army? Like what your job was?" She asks when we've started walking again, the rushing sound of water soothing my tattered emotions.

"My official title was combat engineer, which is a fancy way of saying I made sure the areas we moved through were safe. A lot of surveillance and grounds watch, that sort of thing. My training comes in handy with our security company." There isn't much I can openly share with her but hopefully that's enough.

"Wow. So, you were obviously in a lot of dangerous situations."

I shrug my shoulders in response.

It's Lark's turn to halt our movements before brushing her lips along my cheek. "I'm so glad you made it home safely, Rowen."

I seal my mouth over hers and desire for more rushes through me. I need her love, patience, and understanding along with her gorgeous curves. Lark seems to be easily handing over everything I crave and want. She's the end all.

Our moment is broken when a series of high-pitched moans

echo around us. The distinct sound comes from our right, near the neighbor's house. The shrill noise rings out again and my head snaps in that direction. My body shakes as the laughter bubbles out of me.

Brittany and Nathan, the couple from last night, are going at it—hardcore—against a tree not far from where we're standing. Lark sees them too and slaps a hand over her mouth to keep a cackle from breaking free. There isn't much to see since the dude's body is so massive but there's plenty to hear.

"Holy shit, they're *really* enjoying the great outdoors." Lark snorts as humor shines in her warm caramel eyes.

"Shh, they're going to hear us," I utter while dragging her in the opposite direction, toward the path upstream. We stumble along, trying not to crack up from witnessing their X-rated show. Soon enough the river's splashing current is all that greets our ears.

I'm still laughing when we pause along the bend. "Don't they have a kid with them? He can't still be sleeping."

Lark rolls her eyes. "He's probably napping. They have to get creative and use their time wisely, right? Good for them."

It's great to know she thinks that way. "Maybe we should take notes for when our little ones arrive." I suggest after pulling her sexy figure against me by her belt loop. "It will be helpful down the road."

Lark makes a strangled choking noise before slapping a hand to my chest.

"Whoa, pump the brakes. What guy is desperate for kids? Don't you want to just have sex without responsibility? Children shouldn't be a thought in your mind." Her wide eyes are searching mine, for what I'm not really sure.

"Oh, Vix." I start while nuzzling her neck. "Clearly, I'm not like most men. The sooner I get a ring on your finger and my baby in your belly, the better. I'm romantic like that." More laughter bursts out of me at the stunned expression on her face.

"Seriously, who are you? Did you actually come from a land far, far away? Once upon a time?"

"Nah, just for you. This is a sensitive side you've managed to yank out of me."

Lark lifts a skeptical brow but doesn't argue more. Her face softens suddenly as she lifts a palm to my cheek and I lean into her touch. "I'm sorry for being distant and cold to you at first. I had no idea you were so serious about us. I love you very much, Casper."

"I love you too, Sweetheart. And don't worry, you have the rest of our lives to make it up to me. Speaking of, what are the chances you'll be moving in with me when we get back to the cities?"

"What?" She sputters. "We just started dating! You're constantly going against the norm and it's messing with me. Don't get me wrong, I'm glad you're not afraid of getting serious but this is off the charts." Her hands flail in the air with her exasperation.

I loop my arms around her waist before drawing her into a snug embrace. "Sweetheart, you know this was never just dating." I murmur near her ear. Lark bites her bottom lip before sucking the plump flesh into her mouth. The sight makes me hum happily.

Mine.

"I do know but it's mind boggling that you're the one rushing into all of this. That's supposed to be my job. I've always been the clinger and the pleaser." Her breathy confession is muttered into my chest.

My palms stroke along her back while I respond. "Sweetheart, there is no rulebook for our relationship. We're in this together and that's what matters. Please cling to me. I'd love nothing more." The words are sincere and spoken directly from my heart.

Lark glances up at me through lowered lashes. "Well, my lease is up in a little over a month. Maybe we can talk more about it then."

"There's no maybe, baby. You want to wake up next to me

every morning, right? Go to sleep wrapped around each other?"

Her hesitation melts away when she whispers, "Yes."

"Great. I'm glad that's settled." I smile down at her beautiful face.

Lark returns my joy with a grin so bright, the sight might blind me. I'd happily accept that image as my last.

"So, what should we do now?" She asks coyly, a blush blooming on her cheeks.

"You're thinking dirty thoughts, aren't you? My little vixen is ready to purr some more," I breathe against her glossy pout.

Lark's amber orbs flare and seem to glow. Her chin tilts up for a kiss that I gladly provide. When our lips seal and mouths open, our tongues glide together smoothly like a perfectly practiced dance. Lark breaks away far too soon but the sultry look she flashes at me has my cock jerking in anticipation.

"Lead the way, Vix. I'll follow you anywhere you want to go."

NINETEEN

Lark

S everal weeks have flown by in a flurry of epic orgasms and whirlwind romance. Every second with Rowen is like a dream come true, and I can't believe doubt ever plagued my mind. He's constantly going out of his way to impress me and I'm falling deeper each day. My once empty heart is now bursting with love that refuses to be contained, and why should it be? I want to scream loudly from the rooftops that fairy tales truly do exist and Rowen is living proof.

With every surprise visit to my office or creative date that takes serious planning or whispered words of love, my heart surrenders that much more. And don't even get me started on the sex—sweet mother of everything holy. This man knows what he's doing.

I've been slowly balancing the scale so my job no longer runs my life. Rowen manages to drag me out of work before sunset and further spoils me by cooking dinner. Relief constantly crashes into me each time he reminds I'm no longer alone and there's someone waiting for me to get home. Pretty sure I'm completely moved into his house, with little reluctance on my part, even though my lease isn't up yet. I don't want to deny him anything—why would I?

Rowen is yanking out all my best parts and making them sparkle. His stare is always soul deep and burns through my polished appearance, leaving me exposed and vulnerable for him. I love the cherished look in his bright blues whenever he gazes my way. He's brought my confidence back so cowering behind a façade is no longer needed. He accepts me, and loves me, exactly the way I am. Rowen is legitimately Prince Charming brought to life and all mine.

All these whimsical feelings are being magnified as I help Willow prepare for her wedding. The big day is tomorrow and we arrived at the cabin earlier today to get everything ready. Her younger sister, Wren, was able to catch an earlier flight from Wyoming and has been an enormous help. The three of us make a fantastic crafting team and having some girl time has been great. My friend has been talking nonstop about happily ever after and finding true love, which releases all the blissful butterflies in my belly. I can finally understand what she's been going on about all these months.

We're walking through the woods to some special place Willow and Xander chose to get married. All I see are enormous trees along this path but she keeps telling us to wait and see. Wren is shuffling quietly along next to me. When I glance her way, she spins a finger near her temple to show what she thinks about Willow's plans.

After we walk through an especially dense portion of the forest, a clearing appears and I stop dead in my tracks. "Holy crap," I mutter under my breath.

"Told you so," Willow sing-songs as she skips into the center of this magical space.

Natural sunlight pours through the overhead branches, causing the ground to glisten and glow. My eyes wildly scan the small area as my chest tingles with peace. It's like being lifted up into a mythical dimension where only happiness exists. The blissful calm floats around me like a sweetly scented fog. A small creek runs along the edge and the rush of water provides a Utopian soundtrack.

Wren speaks up next to me. "Yeah, I take back my grumblings about having to hike out here. Totally worth it."

"Willow, this place is fantastic. No wonder you fell in love here," I manage to say while still caught up in the otherworldly illusion before me.

She snickers lightly, the noise full of pure joy. "Isn't it something? I had the same reaction when Xander first showed me."

I spend far too long walking around the property, investigating each inch, as though an invisible force is pushing me along. Eventually, I realize Willow and Wren are working on something I'm probably supposed to help with. I wander over to the pile of rocks they've created in the center of the serene space.

"What's the plan, ladies?" I ask.

Willow's green gaze locks on me. "I don't want to decorate or ruin the organic beauty at all. But I was thinking we could create an aisle of some sort with these." She gestures to the mound of stones by her feet. "Something simple without disrupting the land too much."

I nod while picturing the rustic walkway. "That will be perfect, Willow. I love it. Plus, every bride needs to walk down the aisle."

"Exactly!" She squeals and claps energetically. "You guys, I am so excited. Thank you for helping." She squeezes me in a tight hug before embracing her sister.

I collect a few smooth stones and get started. "How's the Wild West treating you, Wren?" I ask while lining up another rock.

Willow's sister plops down on her butt, giving up on the task for a moment. She blows out a heavy breath, an explanation without saying a word. "I'm almost done with college, which is freaking amazing. But following the rodeo circuit is exhausting.

Even though the school accommodates schedules based off the show season, I feel like there is no down time and everything is a rush. Most of my classes are online, which is helpful but it also takes away from the experience. Lately it's been a mess and I need to decide what to do with my life. Like, do I really want to live out of a trailer for nine months of the year?"

I can only offer a shrug with a slight grimace. "Sounds like you've got a lot on your mind. Hopefully this weekend away will help, rather than add to your stress. Do you still enjoy riding or has it become more of a chore? Like something you have to do?"

"*Urgh*, I don't know anymore. It depends on the day. I love my horses and they're extremely talented but it's a ton of work to keep them in performance shape. It's all I do, you know? There's no time for anything else. Willow talks about love and I've got no clue what that's like." Her tone is sad as her shoulders slump.

I lay a hand on her arm. "You're so young though. Now is the time to do whatever you want before getting involved with someone. When it stops making you happy, bail out, you know? If you'd rather just ride for fun so you can enjoy other stuff, do it!"

Wren rolls her eyes and laughs. "Gosh, you're just like Willow. Always giving such sound advice. You must be a great counselor or whatever."

"I guess that's a compliment." I giggle along with her. "Thanks. But seriously. Life is too short, right?"

"Definitely," she murmurs somberly as a shadow crosses her blue gaze.

Before I can ask her about it, Willow pipes up. "I think that's enough. Right, guys?"

I whip my head around to see what she's talking about. She managed to create two perfect rows while I was chatting with Wren. "Wow, that was quick. Call me impressed. What do you think?" I ask her sister.

Wren plasters on a smile but sadness still lingers in her eyes.

"Yup. I agree. Dinner?" Her short response causes Willow to scrutinize with a raised brow.

"You alright, sis?"

Wren shoos her concern away. "Of course. Don't worry about me. This weekend is all about you and Xander."

Willow doesn't seem convinced but doesn't press her. "All right. Lucky for you two I stocked the house with food. Otherwise we'd be eating beans and beef jerky." She laughs as we start heading back.

Once the pizza is in the oven, the three of us gather around the table to make the daisy halos we'll wear tomorrow. It's quiet while we weave stems and trim leaves so my mind wanders to Rowen. I saw him this morning before heading up here but a pang of longing already resounds in my chest. He grumbled about not sleeping without me next to him but he'll survive one night. I'm not so sure about me though.

"What are you smiling about?" Wren asks.

I look to Willow, assuming she's talking about her, but find my friend staring at me. "Huh?" I question dumbly.

"You're definitely thinking about a man. You look exactly like Willow when she's thinking about Xander." Wren giggles as she points at me.

Willow chuckles too. "My dear friend has fallen in love."

My cheeks heat with their attention locked on me, but I'm not embarrassed to admit my feelings. "Sure am. You'll meet him tomorrow, Wren. He's one of Xander's friends from the clinic."

"That's how you two met?" She wonders while resting her chin on an open palm, clearly ready for a long story.

"Actually no. Rowen and I knew each other before. Well, kind of. Years and years ago he came into the restaurant I was working at. It was just a moment but he disappeared before we could explore it. The first time I saw him again was their," I motion to Willow, "engagement party."

"Ooooh, this has dramatic romance stamped all over it. Tell. Me. Everything." Wren emphasizes her desire for details as her irises sparkle with joy.

When I'm finishing relaying all the mush and goo that is Rowen and my fairy tale love-fest, Wren sighs happily with a smirk on her face. "Lucky bitches. Both of you." Her gaze swings to her sister. "Speaking of happy relationships, how is Xander doing lately? I know he's been spending a lot more time with his parents, which is great."

It's Willow's turn to release a relaxed exhale. "I love him so much, you guys. When we started planning our big day, I suggested doing something with just the two of us. That way he wouldn't be nervous with others around, you know? But Xander refused and told me our families needed to be there. He also came up with using our clearing for the ceremony, which is obviously perfect." A goofy grin forms while she stares off into space, picturing her hubby-to-be I'm sure.

"He's so wonderful, which I already knew, but he's doing so many amazing things for others. He's recently started facilitating his own group at the VA and regularly visits his mom to help her around the house. Their bond snapped back together pretty quickly once he started therapy. He missed her, his dad too, but there's something special about the motherly bond. You know how devastated she was after visiting him here." We both nod in understanding before she continues. "She told me once, when Xander and I were young, how excited she was to dance with him at our wedding someday." Willow sniffles a bit before wiping under her eyes. "Tomorrow is that day and I'm so happy."

She clears her throat and attempts to compose herself. "Gosh, I'm getting all weepy already. What's going to happen when it's my turn to read the vows?" She fixes her watery gaze on us, only to find Wren and me in a similar emotional state. "Oh no, we're going to be a bunch of sobbing Sallys."

We all share a laugh before I ask, "Did you write your own vows?"

"Of course," Willow shoots back with an exaggerated eye roll.

"Then yes, we're all screwed."

»———♡———→

I ADMIRE MY friend as she spins in place, which lifts the skirt of her dazzling dress.

"Holy shit, Willow. You're stunning. That gown is truly something else. Xander won't know what to do with himself." I breathe out while appraising her radiant figure.

She sends me an admonishing glare. "Lark, it's my wedding day. Can you keep the swearing down to a minimum?" Then she lights up like it's Christmas morning. "Oh my gosh! It's my wedding day!" Willow shrieks. "Say whatever you want. Who cares. I'm getting married!"

I toss my head back with a short laugh before getting serious again. "Really, truly though. You're the most beautiful bride I've ever seen."

Willow smiles shyly while checking out the finished product in a nearby mirror, adding another twirl before standing still.

Her cream lace dress sweeps the wood floor. The mermaid style shows the right amount of curves while keeping it elegant. The row of buttons lining Willow's spine took painstakingly long to loop but the effort was well worth it. Her makeup is classically simple, just light dustings of color along her eyes and cheeks, exactly where it counts. All of her long brown hair has been curled in perfect ringlets, which cascade over her left shoulder. A crown of daisies rests on her head to complete the sensational look.

I tried convincing Willow to rock a stellar ruby lip but she refused. Telling me it would get all over when Xander kissed her. The thought caused gleeful flutters to erupt in my belly while a blissful sigh escaped. Today will be a spectacular celebration.

I can't wait to see the look on Xander's face. He's really is going to freak the eff out because even I want to whisk Willow away.

Wren sashays out of the bathroom in a tight-fitting gown that matches mine. The deep purple compliments her tan complexion and I imagine she must drive all the cowboys crazy. Maybe one will manage to snag her heart soon enough. She catches me staring and casts a grin my way.

"Keep looking at me like that and Rowen is going to have some competition." Wren winks before gushing all over her sister, just like I did moments ago.

While they hug and sniffle, I spread my signature red stain on my lips and adjust the ring of flowers in my golden hair. A smirk reflects in the mirror as I imagine Rowen wearing my color on his mouth after we share a passionate kiss. Shivers rush along my skin and I can almost feel his breath fan against my neck. But I shrug it off and turn back to Willow and Wren to join in their exuberance.

After all the compliments are given and emotional babble is exchanged, I send Rowen a text letting him know we're ready. The guest list is small so the event will be intimate, mostly comprised of very close family and friends. Willow and Wren's parents are waiting outside to walk with us. They made sure the guys stayed away and didn't see us before the wedding. When we open the door, the older couple have beaming smiles lighting up their features. It's definitely going to be a day to remember.

The summer weather today is absolutely ideal. The air is warm but a gentle breeze keeps it from getting too hot. Fluffy clouds dot the clear blue sky, providing a picturesque backdrop. I tilt my head toward the sun and let the rays heat my skin. I love everything about this morning already but it's about to get even better.

As we near the clearing, sizzling anticipation slithers up my back. Rowen told me he's wearing a suit and the thought alone set my heart into a frenzy. This entire experience makes me realize just how ready I am to marry him. Maybe it's crazy fast but he doesn't think so and I threw caution to the wind once I agreed to be his.

I sway into the open space, linking arms with Wren, and my sight immediately latches onto Rowen.

Holy shit, he's gorgeous.

TWENTY

Rowen

oly shit, she's gorgeous.
I'm sure most eyes will be locked on the bride today but my gaze won't stray from Lark. Her luscious blonde locks are loosely braided over her right shoulder with pink daisies peeking out on top. The dark purple dress clings to her and swishes along the forest floor as she strolls the aisle. The silk looks like flowing liquid as Lark floats toward me. We'd been given strict instructions to stay away from the cabin so I haven't seen her until right now and it was worth the torture of being apart.

Lark's typical shade of red pops from her pout as her blazing brown eyes laser into me. My breathing is ragged and rattles in my chest, which seems to match the rapid rush of the stream behind me. Her pink tongue slides along her painted lip and the seemingly innocent act awakens my inconvenient desire. I bite my own lip in response as my heated gaze continues eating up the sight of her. Lark falters and stumbles slightly but Willow's sister keeps her upright. A natural flush blossoms on her face and my chest swells with happiness. I can't wait to get my hands all over her sexy ass.

My buddy seems ready to jump out of his skin and is probably feeling the same way about being kept away from Willow until now. Xander's jaw is grinding as his fists flex tight. But then his face relaxes instantly as his bride steps into view. A dopey smile replaces the scowl that was present a second ago and I silently chuckle at his reaction. We are so whipped over our women and it's fucking amazing.

I watch Willow as she slides to her groom but I'm envisioning my little vixen in her place. An anxious ball drops in my gut as I imagine our wedding happening very soon. My eyes almost immediately seek out Lark again, which further sparks my matrimonial feelings. Her stare is focused on her friend but glances my way as if she can feel my gaze. I send her a wink before blowing a kiss, which causes a deeper blush to cover her cheeks. Lark isn't a meek woman but when she gets a bit shy for me, my ego surges with pride.

Xander's father has the honor of marrying the happy couple and my attention turns his way once everyone is in place.

"It is my great privilege to be the one up here between these two wonderful individuals. I've been told by my son to keep it short and sweet so I'll bore you with a longer speech later."

That gets a chuckle from the tiny crowd.

"Willow and Xander have been vital to one another most of their lives. Pretty sure we all knew this day would come eventually. My wife and I are very excited to welcome Willow into our family." He looks at her and smiles wide. "You are an incredible young woman and we are so thankful for you." His eyes get a little glassy before he clears his throat.

Mr. Dixon looks between Willow and Xander before asking, "You've prepared your own vows?" They nod without breaking their intensive stare. "Great. Who's going first?" Xander mutters something that I don't hear but based on his dad's response, he's leading the way.

I sneak a peek at Lark and find her amber gaze latched on me. Love thrums through me at lightning speed and I almost wobble from the blast. My woman has quite the hold on me with just one look. Lark seems affected too based off the tremble in her fingers as she swoops a piece of hair from her forehead. I'd do almost anything to close the gap between us and pour all my feelings into a scorching kiss to her stained lips.

Xander's gruff timbre drags me away from that enticing vision. "I love you, Wills. So fu—effing much it's hard to breathe sometimes," he starts with a hitch in his tone. "I imagined this moment when we first met, baby. As I stared into your bright emerald gaze, and you told me we'd be best friends, I knew you'd be my wife someday. It's no surprise we're standing here now, in front of our loved ones, but this wouldn't have been possible without your strength and determination. You saved me from the darkness, Wills." Xander exhales a shaky breath before clearing his throat. Willow's thumb is continuously rubbing along the top of his hand, as if to soothe any jagged nerves he might be experiencing.

He gives her a little smirk before going on. "I owe you so much, baby. This day wouldn't be possible without you, Wills. *Nothing* would be possible without you.

"Willow, you brought me back to life so I could spend it with you. Because of you, there is a future with endless possibilities we'll explore together. No matter what, I'll be by your side as we travel through this life, and the next one, together. Always. You're the greatest gift I've ever been given and I'm thankful every single day that you agreed to be mine." Xander's volume is low and quiet, as though he'd prefer only Willow hears his words.

The forest is almost completely silent other than the steady flow of a stream nearby. His rapid breathing is like a drumbeat pounding a special tune just for the occasion. It almost seems as if all of us being here is an intrusion. But as he stares at Willow,

Xander appears to be exactly where he wants to be. The overwhelming devotion and adoration pouring from them causes my eyes to mist over before I can blink the emotion away.

Willow is a blubbering mess after Xander's vows so she takes a few deep breaths before attempting to speak.

"I love you, X," she sobs while her sister hands over more tissue. "Today I give my heart, soul, and body to you. Everything I am belongs to you. Now and forever. I've always loved you but on this day, I announce it to our family and friends. I promise to always be everything you need, whenever and wherever, every moment for the rest of our lives," Willow whimpers through quivering lips.

Her words are barely intelligible but that doesn't stop her. "Anywhere our journey leads us, we'll be together. You'll always be my husband and I'll always be your wife. You are my entire reason for living, X. Thank you for coming back to me." Willow swallows audibly while more tears track down her face. "I dedicate and devote my life to loving you."

Xander moves to her until they're locked in a tight embrace. Willow's shoulders are shuddering while he whispers against her glistening cheek. Witnessing their irreplaceable bond in such raw form has my heart spasming as I glance at Lark. Her watery gaze lifts to mine and a wobbly smile tilts her lips. I know she feels it too. When I look back at Willow and Xander, their trembling fingers are accepting the rings that solidify their union. Although no symbols are needed to comprehend their undying love.

While they share their first kiss as husband and wife, I rush toward Lark and wrap her in my arms. She collapses against me before sliding her hands around my waist. We stand motionless for a few long moments, the outpouring of adoration and devotion surrounding us, while I silently image tying the knot with this beautiful woman. The significance of this day is more than just celebrating an amazing couple—although that's why we've all come together. For me, it's about appreciating and understanding the importance of finding that one special person. And I most certainly have. I allow my sappy thoughts to soak into our connection. I kiss the top of her head while murmuring, "I love you, Sweetheart."

Lark lifts her face from my chest and whispers back, "I love you so much, Rowen." And that's all we need to say.

As we separate slightly, I slip my palm into hers before bringing her soft skin to my lips. Lark sighs happily and squeezes her fingers along mine. We walk the aisle together as others begin to leave the clearing. I take another look around as we head for the path. This place could make the most negative cynic believe in love. The ground practically vibrates with the romantic emotion. If I wasn't already crazy about Lark and planning our future, this little slice of heaven would do the trick.

"Isn't this a beautiful spot?" she breathes out as we walk, our connected hands swing between us.

I hum in agreement and nod. "It really is. Makes me want to get married, Sweetheart."

Lark glances at me from the corner of her eye and smirks. "Seems anything has that impact on you."

A light chuckle rumbles in my chest. "Because of you, Vix. Never thought I would feel this way until you stomped back into my life."

"I did not stomp." She scoffs.

"You most certainly did." I laugh again while recalling her sassy attitude that night in the bar.

"Whatever, Casper," Lark grumbles.

I lift her hand to my mouth and brush a kiss along her smooth wrist. "Look how far we've come."

Her amber irises sear into me as she says, "And in such a short amount of time."

"That's because we're meant to be, Sweetheart."

"You managed to restore my faith in soul mates. I didn't think it was possible."

"Happy to prove you wrong, Vix."

Lark snickers. "Such a charmer."

We arrive in the cabin's backyard, which has been transformed for the reception. Xander told me he was surprising Willow with the decorations, and based off their cuddle against the shed, I'd say she was very pleased. They probably won't waste much time with us before finding somewhere more private.

Xander strung up a bunch of lights around the perimeter so the small area glows as the sun is beginning to set. Tables piled with food and beverages are along one side while a makeshift dance floor takes up a large portion near the house. The picnic tables and benches Xander made have been randomly placed along the edges so I lead Lark over to an empty seat.

"Want something to eat or drink?" I ask after she settles in.

Her brown eyes glitter as she looks up at me. "Surprise me, Casper."

If only Lark knew everything I've been planning. This weekend has been giving me plenty of shock-value inspiration.

TWENTY ONE

Lark

This entire day has been an explosion of fairy tale romance and I couldn't be happier as we watch the newlyweds share their first dance. My spirit soars as Xander spins Willow around and around, showing her off with a beaming smile on his face. These two should be spokesmodels for finding your one true love. My stomach almost aches with how sweet the sight is.

When I glance at Rowen across the yard, my belly flip-flops as I catch his sparkling gaze devouring me. He's talking to Xander's dad but I'm not sure their conversation is mutual at the moment. The deep charcoal suit fits his broad frame perfectly and I can't wait to peel each stitch of fabric off later. The black tie around his neck is already loosened and several creative uses begin pinging in my brain. My lower belly tightens in excitement as my skin prickles.

"Holy shit, you weren't joking about that guy," Wren whispers over my shoulder, startling me a bit. She laughs at my expression. "Lost in the moment?"

I turn to look at her before lifting a brow. "Right? My man is crazy hot."

"So jelly. They don't have them like that in Wyoming." She mutters.

A giggle escapes me as I imagine the cowboys Wren is usually surrounded by. "Rowen is definitely one of a kind, but I'm sure there's a man out there waiting for you, just got to look for him."

She rolls her eyes. "Maybe all this sugary sap is going to my head. You guys are cramming it down my throat everywhere I go." Her scoff is exaggerated. "Once I get back home, the withdrawal will be painful. But I'll be too busy to care, right? My life's indecision continues on a constant loop." Wren squints at her sister with a pursed pout.

Before I can respond, Rowen sneaks up and pulls me into his bulky body. "What are you ladies talking about? Me, I hope," he murmurs close to my ear.

Shivers race down my spine at how close we're pressed together. I can feel his slight bulge against my hip. "Always, Casper," I whisper back after nuzzling into his neck.

"This is exactly what I'm talking about. There's no escape!" Wren huffs before crossing her arms, as if that will protect her from the lovefest she's swimming in.

Rowen's chuckle puffs against an especially sensitive patch of my skin, causing another shock of tremors to attack my system. He buzzes his lips gently along the same spot and I fall further into him.

"Mind if I steal my girl away, Wren?" He asks before continuing his assault on my nape.

"Please, by all means. I've seen plenty." She laughs while waving us away.

"Dance with me, Sweetheart?" Rowen growls quietly.

I can only nod while staring deeply into his bottomless ocean gaze. Refusing his requests would never cross my mind, ever again.

He leads us to the dancefloor where others are moving to

a slow beat echoing from a pair of speakers. Rowen twists me around before looping his muscular arms around my waist and hauling me in extra tight. His flat palms roam down until they're resting on my ass. Pretty sure his paws cover me completely, which makes me feel protected by his possessive touch. Wrapped up in Rowen is my favorite place to be.

"Are you not wearing panties, Vix? *Again?*" He asks as his fingers bunch slightly in the fabric of my gown.

"Of course not. Nothing else was fitting under this dress."

He grips me harder, his searing touch sending electric shocks to my core. "I'd love to shove something else under there."

"Oh, I bet you would. Lucky for you, there's a hotel room with our name on it."

"Is it too early to leave? Not sure how long I can wait. Especially now that you told me there's nothing but bare skin under this silk." Rowen groans before thrusting his firm arousal against me. Had I been wearing panties, they'd be reduced to a pile of ashes by now.

I moan softly in return, "Just a little bit longer. Then I'm all yours, all night long."

"*Fuuuuck.*" He grinds out.

I decide to tease Rowen a bit more. "Did you know banging a groomsman is on the top of my bucket list?" I purr while rubbing against his stiff length.

His eyes clench shut while he croaks, "Why am I not surprised?"

"What can I say? I love a guy in a suit and with all the passion in the air, it's the perfect combination. Want to help me check that off tonight?" My eyebrows wag suggestively when his vivid blues focus on me again.

Rowen sputters a laugh. "Life goals? At this hour?"

I shrug lightly. "You know me. Always working toward something."

"Speaking of goals, are you going to marry me?"

"Haven't we already been over this? You'll get a lot further if you ask me properly. Don't assume I'm going to say yes no matter what. You know what they say about that . . ." My voice trails off, leaving him to *assume* what I mean.

He ignores my nonsense. "Just tell me what I want to hear, Sweetheart." Rowen presses forward before dipping me over his arm. He nibbles along my collarbone and trails up to my jaw where he sucks softly.

My eyelids flutter shut as I breathe, "Someday, yes."

He pulls me up before lazily spinning us around the floor. "Someday soon, you mean?" Rowen asks but it's not really a question. "What about having all my babies?" He murmurs along my flushed cheek.

"Don't push it, Casper." Humor laces my voice while I inhale his delicious spicy scent. Cinnamon and cedar is a lethal combo, trust me.

"Come on, Vix. Tell me what I want to hear."

This guy with his extreme need to lock me down—I love it.

"*Urgh*, fine. So persistent." Rowen hums in approval. "It would be my honor to have an entire mini-fleet of your gorgeous lady-killer children."

"That's my girl," he replies with a grin while resting his palm against my lower belly, which causes joyful tingles to cover my entire body. Rowen makes me so ridiculously happy. I can't keep the wide smile off my face.

He must catch my glee because a soft chuckle vibrates in his chest. "I knew you'd give into me, Sweetheart."

I push his shoulder lightly. "You gave into me just as much and we both know it"

Rowen keeps laughing. "You're right. So, how about we go master the art of baby-making?" His eyebrows rise suggestively, which has me chuckling too.

"Hmmm, practice does make perfect." I whisper across his scruffy jaw. "But not yet. We need to at least wait for the bride and groom to dip out first." We take a quick peek at the *very* happy couple, currently making out against a tree.

"All right," he breathes while gathering me ridiculously closer, obscenely so for this type of setting. But after a quick glance around, every couple is smashed together in a similar intimate connection.

So much love in the air, and we're part of it.

That happy thought has me snuggling closer into Rowen's solid body, feeling cherished and treasured by this man. He rests his forehead against mine and a light puff of air caresses my neck each time he exhales—the sensation consuming every part of me.

"Thank you," I rasp almost silently.

"For what, Vix?"

My mind races as I attempt to nail down the most important reasons but I can't settle on just a few. *"Everything,"* comes out as a long sigh against his handsome face. "You've given me something to believe in again and saved me from myself." I swallow a few times to collect the emotion before spilling my guts.

"My heart pounds a rhythm I've never known before because it's beating along with yours. Nothing else matters to me except being near you, forever. Forget eating, drinking, and breathing. Just you, Casper." My tone is hoarse as I push through the boulder lodged in my throat. "An invisible thread weaves all around, tying us together for eternity. You're like an uncontrollable urge, a relentless force that takes over, and I'm only calm when we're close. Like this." I squeeze him in my arms as I press against him, until there's absolutely no space between us.

"It's like I'm free falling without a parachute. Will you catch me, Rowen?" I whisper my desire in his ear.

He doesn't hesitate. "Of course, Sweetheart. Always."

"You make my soul smile and laugh. You make me so happy,

it's like I'm constantly soaring yet tethered to you at the same time. You're my forever, Casper."

Rowen brushes a quick kiss along my lips. "You're so fucking amazing, Vix. Especially when you reveal what's truly deep down inside. I love you, Sweetheart. Forever and always."

Flutters erupt in my belly as I close my eyes and lose myself in this moment. "I love you so much," I mumble along his mouth. "Did you ever watch *Friends*?"

"What?" he asks as his face scrunches slightly.

"Seems totally random but there was an episode about finding your lobster. Apparently they mate for life. I always thought it was cute as hell and wanted to use that line." I laugh at my nonsense rambling.

Of course Rowen gets it. "So, I'm your lobster?"

"Well, yes. Although it was proven they don't actually mate for life so it ended up being a huge let down. You're my mate for life, though. Screw the lobsters sleeping around!" I wail as I toss a fist in the air. That gets me a rumbling laugh from Rowen, which gets me cackling too.

What a pair we make.

After the humor dies down, his bright blue stare sears into me as he leans forward for a scorching kiss. Our lips slide together in flawless unison, sucking gently while gliding softly. Mouths open so tongues can explore, licking and lapping with reckless abandon, but we aren't in a hurry. Our kiss is a languid assault as we sway to a smooth melody. My fingers skate up his spine while his palms roam along my ass. Rowen's erection is begging for escape against my pelvis while my nipples are ready to poke through fabric. With a few final strokes and nibbles, we break apart before stopping isn't an option.

Rowen's chest is rising and falling rapidly as his fiery gaze consumes me. That look alone causes my breath to hitch as a pleasurable clench ricochets from my core. He bites his lip before detonating the explosives wired to blast into my hopelessly romantic spirit.

"I'm going to make you Mrs. Sworr real soon, Sweetheart."

TWENTY TWO

Rowen

"Just got off the phone with Brock. I'm so fucking stoked about this expansion, Row. It's huge for us." Linc's brash timbre breaks into my thoughts.

I was wrapped up in visions of Lark, exactly where my mind always wanders, but even more so after the wedding last weekend. Over the last several days, I've been busy making plans. Tonight will be very special. I rub my forehead to get back on track.

We've got to close this deal with our future partner. "I know, bro. I've been scouring this contract and it's legit. This will set us up with some serious flow so we can finally hire a few more guys. All we have to do is sign on the dotted line," I say after reading over the final paragraph again.

"Do you think Croy and Xander are interested?" Lincoln asks while settling into a chair across from my desk.

My younger brother, Croy, is still living in Texas but planning to move back before winter. I met up with him when we were down south making collaborative plans with Brock. He seemed pretty stoked about getting a job at Sworr Security when I mentioned our company growing. I love the kid but he's still a little shit sometimes. This partnership with Brock isn't a long-term guarantee, even though that's exactly what we're gunning for, so I'm still wary about offering Croy a spot.

If this deal goes through, Xander is a definite addition to our team. He's already been helping out with small side jobs when we have them and is ready for plenty more. His discomfort with people, crowds especially, is something he's still working on but he's motivated. He wants to be part of a team again, gain responsibility and purpose, so I'm going to give him that.

"Xander is solid for sure. I gave him a heads up earlier that we're close to sealing everything up. I'm more hesitant with Croy because he's not living up here yet and I don't trust his dumbass to make it happen. I'll call him once the expansion is definite. We don't need to decide about new staff just yet anyway." I respond after thinking shit through. My palms roughly scrub at my face while I decide what to do next.

Linc pipes up before any ideas take root. "How's your girl? Still going good? You've been walking around with your damn head in the clouds all week."

"Lark is doing great, thanks for asking. We've got a date tonight actually. Jealous much?" I taunt.

He scoffs. "Not likely. No woman will ever trap my ass."

"When you meet the right one, you'll be begging her to tie you down . . . If you know what I mean." I wag my eyebrows at him while making a mental note to pick up some rope.

"That's hilarious and you're delusional. We're different, you and me. I never want a wife and 2.5 kids running around, terrorizing my silence. I'm all good with the bachelor life plus a side of sex. I know that honey of yours has some hot friends. Why don't you hook me up?" He asks and thrusts his hips crudely.

"You're such a douche. Grow up. I'd never sacrifice Lark's friends so you can get your dick wet."

A chuckle busts out of him. "They'd be lucky to get a ride

on my ten inches."

Now it's my turn to laugh. "Bullshit, Linc. I've seen your pasty ass naked in the locker room plenty and you'd be lucky to claim six. Tops."

Our worthless banter keeps going until the phone rings, ending our immature shenanigans. After a brief conversation with the real estate agent, I hang up and look at my cousin's questioning face. "That was Bill. He's at the space if you want to tour it again. They cleaned it up since we were there last. Might be worth a gander. We can take new pictures for Brock, give him that final shove."

"Hell yes. We can head out soon and I'll drive. I just have to finish watching some tape from the Walter's party. Such a boring surveillance feed. I want to stab myself in the eyes to get it over with. Pays the bills though, right?" He says as he stands up.

"I'm picking up Lark right after work so I'll take my own car."

Lincoln coughs into his hand, "Pussy whipped."

"Happily," I sing-song back at him.

"You're so lame, dude," he grumbles.

I snicker at his antics. "Seriously? We're doing this again? You just said you've got shit to do."

"Yeah, yeah. You're just trying to get rid of me so you can get back to daydreaming about Lark."

"Exactly, so get the fuck out of here." I wave him off as he leaves my office.

A few hours full of contracts and calls passes before Lincoln is ready to leave. I follow him to the industrial area of downtown where Brock is looking to set up his Minneapolis location. The streets are clogged with afternoon traffic but we make the commute in under thirty minutes. Unfortunately there aren't a lot of big spaces open so I circle the neighboring blocks. Once again I'm reminded that fucking city parking is not equipped to handle my truck.

Bill, the real estate agent, is standing out front with Lincoln as I stroll up. He sticks a hand out in greeting for me to shake. "Hey Rowen." He nods at my cousin before looking back at me. "I was just telling Lincoln about the latest improvements inside. All new everything. I'm glad you two were willing to stop by."

"Thanks for taking time to meet with us, Bill. We appreciate the chance to look at the property again," I say as we walk through the front entrance.

Linc adds, "Definitely. I know Brock is pretty dead set on this place but a few more snapshots won't hurt."

Bill nods his head. "I understand completely. Demo had just finished last time so everything was a mess. Now you can see the layout without all the dust hindering the view."

We walk around the first floor of the empty building, practically a shell just waiting for purpose. The other levels are very similar and we've already seen them before. The wall facing the main street is made entirely of glass, which gives the area a lot of great natural light. Other than plain sheetrock and concrete flooring, the vast space is a blank canvas.

"The seller is motivated and ready to move forward so if your buyer wants it, you better tell him to hurry," Bill says as we make it back to the front door. "I have to meet another client for dinner. Feel free to stick around for a bit and take the pictures you need. Let me know if you need anything in the meantime." He hands me a set of keys for the back door, which has a lockbox, before leaving us to it.

Lincoln uses his cell to capture some images while I text Lark to let her know we'll be done soon. Nerves trickle up my back as I think about what lies ahead for my little vixen this evening. It's a moment we'll never forget, especially if she accepts.

"All set?" Linc asks as we're nearing the rear of the building.

I take one more glance around while envisioning the space all done up and decorated like the company in Texas. "I think so. This works out well, right? Especially or us since it's relatively close and in a decent part of town?" I ask while we step out into the back alley.

This is the one part I don't like. The narrow area isn't lit up well and seems like an endless tunnel either way we turn.

"This shouldn't be an exit, especially at night."

Linc agrees with me, "I hear you. It's eerie as hell. Why aren't there any spotlights?" He laughs and slaps me on the shoulder before backing away. "Don't let the boogie man get you, all right? I'll see you Monday. Have fun on your date, man."

"Yeah, thanks. Have a good one," I call out to his retreating form in the dark.

I grab my phone to call Lark as I'm locking up the heavy door, thankful for the bright bulb hanging overhead. Hurried footsteps sound behind me and I'm sure Lincoln left something behind.

I chuckle and ask over my shoulder, "What'd you forget? Or did you miss me too much?"

A gruff voice barks out, "Give me your fucking wallet. The watch too."

What the fuck?!

Instant fury thunders through me as I spin around on the spot, facing the moron who thinks stealing from me is a good idea. Before I'm able to react, blinding pain rips into my torso and causes me to stumble against the wall. The fucker doesn't think twice before yanking his knife from my side, which sends another round of blistering torture through my body.

Wet warmth oozes from me as I straighten along the concrete. Blood is already seeping into my shirt and spreading fast as the fabric sticks to my gaping flesh.

Fuck.

The wound must be deep to be leaking this quickly. After applying pressure to the nasty injury, I grit my teeth and attempt to ignore the wave of nausea rolling through me.

Who does this idiot think he is?

Then again, no one can see us from the street back here. I'm not sure many can see us at all based on the isolated setup of this alley. His form is twitching slightly as his chin bobs to a rhythm I can't hear. Maybe he's on something and desperate for a fix, figuring he'd jump me for money when I wasn't looking.

Fucking asshole prick.

He stays in the shadows but his silhouette is highlighted by the lamp so I can clearly see when he tries coming at me again. I block his attack easily enough before driving my fist into his jaw, causing him to fall back. The effort takes a toll on my rapidly fading system and black splotches dance in my vision. My eyes clench shut to rid the obstructions from view and I realize the mistake too late as his blade slashes across my abdomen. I'm momentarily stunned by the searing fire blasting through my stomach. A hoarse yell escapes as the excruciating torture causes dizziness to blur my sight again. My knees threaten to buckle from the brutal bone-jarring agony sinking into me but I manage to stay upright.

My right arm bands around my middle while I attempt to fight him off with my left. This shifty-eye guy would normally be no match for me but he fucking blindsided me. When I aim for his nose with my palm, the movement is sluggish so he dodges before sinking his jagged knife into my exposed shoulder and twisting aggressively. A tormented roar tears up my throat as everything gets fuzzy. I drop to my knees when my legs can no longer support my weight. Weakness vibrates throughout me as I begin fading faster. I collapse to the ground and groan as my injuries split wider. The front of my shirt is sopping and plastered to my battered body.

Shouting echoes into the silence but quickly fades around me, sounding very far away. Maybe it's not even real. My mind is getting foggy as the sweltering pain rakes over each piece of me. The crunch of footsteps get closer and hope for survival blooms.

Lincoln better catch this fucking guy.

As I'm drifting into unconsciousness, images of my little vixen waiting for me flicker before my fluttering eyelids. I picture Lark cursing up a storm for standing her up, which has me fighting to stay awake in spite of all this shit. She's going to be so disappointed when I don't show up.

I'm still coming for you, Sweetheart.

My last thought before blackness consumes me is of Lark finding the ring in my pocket.

TWENTY THREE

Lark

"So, you really think it's going to happen tonight?" Willow asks again for the fifth time in an hour.

An aggravated groan bubbles out. "I don't want to talk about it anymore. I'm afraid of jinxing it," I grumble from my spot along the gymnasium wall.

Willow huffs and rolls her eyes. "Says the woman who didn't believe in fate or destiny two months ago. Just tell me why you have that gut feeling?"

"Rowen has been more secretive than usual. Making calls out of the room and brushing me off when I ask about it. That's not like him, *at all*. He always tells me whatever I want to know." Frustration prickles my scalp just thinking about it. "Plus, Rowen's been planning something for this evening but won't give me any details. Other than he'll pick me up and I need to wear the red dress from your engagement party. He was *very* specific about that." We share a laugh because that outfit has only ever been worn with a *very* certain goal in mind.

As if suddenly realizing we're in the gym alone, Willow screws up her face while spinning around in place. "Where the heck did everyone go?"

There was a decent team of us still at work but Cindy snagged the others to help with a parent concern. I'd much rather pick up balls and bases on a Friday afternoon close to quitting time.

Heh, balls.

"They left a while ago. How did you just notice?" I shoot her a funny look.

She gestures wildly between us. "We were talking about you and Rowen getting married. I was rightfully distracted."

I point at her accusingly. *"You* were trying to bring it up, and not so subtly. I never said we're getting married."

Willow scoffs. "Whatever. It was implied by your womanly intuition and Rowen's wacky behavior. Plus, that man is crazy about you and will most definitely be getting down on one knee."

I'd never admit it but her reassurance has excitement rushing through me. Nothing would be greater than Rowen proposing but I refuse to get my hopes up. Someday he will, for sure, but I won't assume it's happening this quickly. No matter how many times he asks me in that casual way of his.

Rowen texted earlier about being done with work soon and my heart almost burst with anxiety. He's going to be picking me up in a few short hours. My palms get clammy imaging what lies ahead. What if he really plans on . . .

A sudden hip check bumps me out of my reverie.

"You're picturing it right now, aren't you? I can tell. Totally spaced out." Willow waves a hand in front of me before I bat her away.

"Shouldn't you be on a honeymoon or something?" I snap impatiently while crossing my arms.

My friend sighs wistfully. "Every day is like a vacation with Xander. We don't need to jet off somewhere tropical to celebrate our love."

"Wow, that's actually really sweet," I tell her honestly.

"You wouldn't have said that a few months ago," Willow snickers.

My gaze drops with the reminder of my shitty attitude. "I was such a bitch. For defensive and protective reasons, but still. How did you handle me?"

"Very carefully. And with a lot of booze. I also stayed out of your way, but you were always working so it wasn't that hard."

"Oh my God, I wasn't that horrible!" My voice rises in offense.

Willow snorts. "Jeez, just teasing. But Rowen has been the best thing to ever happen to you. For real."

The mention of his name brings a surge of heat to my lower belly as a smirk tilts my lips. "He certainly is. I'm not afraid to admit it."

"Thank goodness for that, chica. You needed a swift kick in the butt to reset that backwards thinking. Love is grand." She snips when my snarky eyebrow arcs up, "Don't look at me that way. I'm being ridiculous on purpose."

"Uh huh. Well, this discussion has been super enlightening but I have a date to get ready for. What are you two doing tonight?" I ask as we start walking back to our offices.

Willow's grin lights up her face. "Xander wants to see a movie at the discount theater. They're playing something we saw together in high school."

"That's way too cute."

"I know, right? And it's never going to wear off."

"Oh, I believe it. You guys will still be sucking face in the old folks' home like horny teenagers." We giggle at the thought and pause outside my door.

Her hands grip my shoulders after she turns toward me, a watery glint reflects in her emerald eyes. "It's going to happen. You know it and so do I. Will you call me? Right away?" Willow sniffs lightly while wiping under her eyes, her voice wobbling a bit. "I love you like a sister and am truly happy Rowen came back into your life. I'm emotionally invested in what happens because you're both close to me." She blubbers in near hysterics.

My arms wrap around her waist in a tight hug, making sure to pour some extra sugar into the embrace.

"I love you too, Willow. Thank you for always being here for me and calling me on my crap. I really appreciate it." I tilt my head and assess her tears. "Pretty sure you'll be more upset than me when he doesn't ask," I joke.

"Is that sarcasm? Not the time, Lark . . ." She sticks her tongue out before turning to her office. "All right, no more emotion overload." Willow glances over her shoulder and gives me the weakest case of puppy dog eyes I've ever seen. "Lark, will you really call me?"

I roll my eyes playfully. "Of course. When Rowen actually proposes, you'll be one of the first to know."

She winks and waves before strolling away. Our goofy conversation distracts me temporarily but then I'm alone and the nerves wash back over me like a cold shower. My skin prickles with goosebumps as a shiver ripples through me.

I might get engaged tonight.

Those words continue to ping around my brain as I drive home. That statement keeps me company in the shower. The potential derails my concentration as I'm getting ready and it takes three tries before my hair is plaited in a perfect fishtail braid. My fingers tremble as I apply my bright ruby shade to my lips. The zipper of my dress snags when I image Rowen dragging it down later. My mind whirls with endless possibilities until I'm finally ready—just in time—at exactly eight o'clock.

But my boyfriend isn't here.

I expect Rowen to be waiting like usual, since he's always early, but his sexy smirk is nowhere in sight. Figures the one time I'm punctual, he's running late. I laugh at the irony after shooting him a quick text, then browse social media while leaning against the kitchen counter.

After fifteen minutes, Rowen still hasn't shown up or responded to my messages. I'm sure there's a very good reason he's not here but worry creeps up my spine regardless. Pouring a tall glass of red wine calms my fraying nerves and the first hearty gulp gives me a reality check. Sometimes Rowen will be behind schedule, it's totally acceptable and doesn't mean anything other than he has a busy day at work.

As another stream of time trickles by without word from him, and my intentions of remaining level headed begin crumbling. My glass has been drained and my entire body seems to be covered in edgy jitters. The toxic insecurity that once plagued me tries seeping into the cracks but I shove the desire to withdraw away.

Rowen wouldn't do that to me.

My stilettos clack on the floor when my legs refuse to remain still anymore. I begin aimlessly wandering around my apartment imagining the worst but wishing for something stupidly simple. Rowen will be here soon with a perfect explanation of what held him up even though I won't ask. All I really need is for him to storm in and wrap me in his protective embrace.

One hour morphs into two and my anxiety ratchets up, practically strangling me. I've been trying to stay calm without overreacting or shutting down but it's difficult when that's my automatic defense. I've called Rowen at least ten times and left just as many messages when his voicemail was the one to pick up. A slew of unanswered texts have been sent but I fire off another just in case he answers this time.

> Me: *Casper, it's been over two hours and I'm seriously freaking out. Just let me know what's going on.*

Tremors attack my hands, even after I shake them out vigorously. The pacing resumes, back and forth then back again. Painful cramps attack my stomach, clenching brutally before releasing; the sensation feels like I'm being stabbed. My mind is spinning faster than I can keep up with as a wicked spell of dizziness threatens to clobber me.

Fuck.

Fuck, fuck, fuck!

My heels stomp with each explicative. I grab my phone and call Willow but she doesn't answer either. The panic shaking my voice is obvious as I leave her a near-hysteric message. My skin is crawling with suspicion so my nails drag along any exposed flesh to distract me from the eerie feeling. Fear pierces my scalp and slowly slithers down my entire form before settling in my tingling toes.

My vision swims and my chest seems to be caving in under the weight of the unknown. I can't give up though, not again. *Never again.* The anxiety zaps through me like lightning as my heart rate skyrockets. Suddenly the signs of a panic attack are looming and threatening to steal the air from my lungs.

What's happening?

I didn't push him into anything. Exactly the opposite. Rowen was always the aggressor when it came to our future, which is why confidence beats like a bass drum inside of my brain. The booming noise is almost powerful enough to silence the familiar pang of rejection but a few nasty thoughts barrel through.

Did I cling too hard?

Hope too much?

Did he realize we've been moving too fast?

Shit. Fucking shit.

My inner strength screams louder in response, effectively muting the taunting destruction.

No! No, dammit.

Rowen wouldn't do that. He loves me and I feel his genuine devotion within the furthest depths of my being, cuddling around my soul like the softest blanket. Something else must have happened, and those possibilities terrify me even more.

Who the hell can I call?!

When my cell begins vibrating, I almost drop it in desperation to answer as my chest squeezes brutally in anticipation.

I raise the phone to my ear before nearing screaming, "Hello?!"

An unknown woman's voice calmly responds. "Hello ma'am. Is this Lark Somers?"

My trembling hand causes the device to wobble. "Yes. Yes, this is she. Who's this?"

She ignores my questions but gives truth to my worst fear. "You're listed as Rowen Sworr's emergency contact and he was emitted to Percy Hospital earlier this evening. He just got out of surgery—"

Before she says more, the phone clatters to the ground as I run to my car.

TWENTY FOUR

Rowen

Beep.

Beep-beep. Beep-beep.

That's what wakes me during these short stints of semi-lucidness. I don't know where I am or what that noise indicates, but it jolts me out of the silent darkness.

The bout of awareness starts with floating.

My body is warm and tingling everywhere but I can't move. It's like I'm suspended above the ground without explanation, as though I'm trapped between this life and the next. I know I'm not dead because pain begins filtering in.

The sensation is dull at first, like an pinch in my chest I can't rub away or a clench in my gut that won't ease. Without warning, it's like the fog is lifted as my body becomes engulfed in flames. Everything burns but I can't escape the fire. Hours pass where is seems I'm baking beneath the sun after being deserted in Death Valley.

Suddenly I'm doused in ice cold water and trapped in a freezer. My teeth seem to be chattering as my fingers and toes go numb. That paralyzing insensitivity must mean the end is near and panic seeps into my frozen form. I'm losing any feeling in my detached body and freaking the fuck out. My bones throb from the effort of trying to flee but getting nowhere. My muscles trained for combat strain and pull but nothing happens.

I try screaming but no sound comes out. My throat is parched from thirst but I can't move to drink anything. Metallic sawdust coats my mouth and my lips sting from being so dry. My eyelids seem sewn shut and I can't break the seal. They won't lift so I'm trapped in endless black as my hope wanes.

The noises become more insistent and frequent, like alarm bells blaring. The beeping is faster and a low buzz pulses in my ears. Piercing light swoops into my vision, sending sharp pain into my skull and ending the vast nothingness. My lungs must be working as I manage to suck in gasps of air while shooting agony hammers into me.

During these brutal moments, I try picturing Lark and the pure joy she always injects into me. Her form is distorted and blurry but she eases the suffering slightly. Once I think of her, I need her close. My body radiates distress for an entirely different reason. I would gladly accept this type of misery if it meant she's nearby. I'm desperate to grasp onto the fuzzy images of Lark.

My lifeline.

My reason for existing.

My everything.

These thoughts cause my heart to jackknife as the desire to have her with me becomes frantic. In my mind, I'm thrashing violently in reckless determination to reach her. I can't be sure what's actually happening and that causes my hysteria to intensify. The pressure in my head is like an unyielding vice but I can't stop fighting when Lark might be close. Maybe if I keep pushing myself, I can reach her. If only my hand could lift and cup her silky cheek, peace would flow through my fiery veins.

When a soothing sensation sails through me, my racing pulse

immediately slows. A pleasantly warm blast of bliss starts at my fingertips and zips up my arm before settling into my pounding chest. These are the moments I imagine Lark is beside me, clutching my hand. Unexpected exhaustion slams into me once my body is calm. My thoughts turn spotty and sluggish, like I'm being dragged under water and away from the surface. Just as suddenly as all these sensations appear, they melt into a pool of nothingness with a few sporadic sounds.

Beep.

Beep-beep. Beep-beep.

Before I can contemplate any of this bizarre shit, the weight gets too heavy and yanks me back under.

TWENTY FIVE

Lark

R owen is hurt.
  He's in the hospital.
  He needs me.
These truths play on a continuous loop as I approach the emergency room parking ramp after a seriously questionable journey since my focus is scattering with the passing wind. The drive flies by as I whizz down the empty streets, thankful beyond belief that my apartment is so close. I barely remember getting to my car before having to run back upstairs for my keys and phone which I carelessly left behind. The nurse I'd spoken to couldn't tell me much, other than Rowen had been seriously injured, and just got out of surgery. I will know the rest soon enough.

My blurry eyes keep leaking as I stumble into the bustling lobby but luckily the information desk isn't hard to find. When the receptionist tells me only immediate family are allowed to visit, the lie about being Rowen's wife easily rolls off my tongue. She raises a skeptical brow as she takes in my distraught appearance but must decide I look the part. Her pursed lips tell me the way before she points in his general direction.

At least I was smart enough to ditch the heels because these slippery floors are a serious hazard. My flats allow me to run without any further issues other than the constant stream of tears pouring down my face.

After finding the room, I pause for a single breath and gather my courage, even though I want to be a weepy puddle on the floor. When I open the door, my knees threaten to buckle at the sight of Rowen's unconscious form lying on the bed. A sob breaks free before I can stop it, but I clasp a trembling palm over my mouth to mute the broken whimper.

My feet shuffle silently as I quietly edge toward him, not wanting to disturb his peaceful slumber. The closer I get to his side, the more obvious it becomes that he's knocked out. Rowen's facial features are completely relaxed, his forehead smooth and jaw slack. He's mostly covered by a thin white sheet but the bandages wrapped around his upper body are still apparent. My vision swims as I continue staring and picturing what's hidden underneath. The gentle rise and fall of Rowen's torso locks me in a trance as I settle into a chair near his bed.

I barely hear the soft knock behind me. "Mrs. Sworr?" The question is whispered but still startles me and I practically fall out of my seat.

After quickly glancing over my shoulder at the man standing in the doorway, my eyes scan around the room looking for Rowen's mother. When my gaze settles on the stranger again, I realize he's talking to me. My mind trips on the term until I remember why he's calling me that.

I nod while responding softly, "Yes, that's me."

He steps further into the room before introducing himself. "I'm Dr. Richmond, the doctor on call tonight." His tone is kind and genuine, making me feel a sliver of comfort.

We shake hands briefly—and awkwardly—since I'm still freaking the eff out internally.

Something horrible happened to Rowen, like really fucking bad, and he's still lying motionless in recovery. My eyelids flutter before closing completely, the weight of this situation becoming too much.

Dr. Richmond clears his throat before diving in. "I'm sure you have a lot of questions, Mrs. Sworr. The most important thing to know is that Rowen is expected to make a full recovery. He's young and healthy, which benefits him immensely. The multiple stab wounds—"

I gasp audibly.

" . . . To his abdomen and shoulder caused a lot of blood loss. His spleen was damaged and his lung was punctured, that's why it was necessary to operate." He explains calmly while my misery washes down my cheeks. Dr. Richmond's face pinches slightly before he keeps going. "There was a significant spike in his temperature, which lead us to believe more was going on. We caught the infection quickly, before the bacteria could spread. Thankfully his cousin found him right away and called an ambulance, otherwise Rowen's condition could have been far worse."

A loud cry bubbles from me before I can trap it and the doctor pauses in understanding. The gears in my brain are grinding in an attempt to keep up with all the complicated information tossed my way. It's all too much. My head drops as another round of tears flow, my entire body shakes from the overwhelming emotion.

"I think that's enough for now. It's a great thing you're here for him. Feel free to stay right where you are," The doctor says while I try getting a grip on myself.

Between sniffles I manage to ask, "How long will he be sleeping?"

Dr. Richmond grabs Rowen's chart. "Looks like he was given a pretty hefty sedative to keep him resting through the night. Rowen might not regain consciousness until tomorrow afternoon depending on his blood pressure and fever. His body went through severe trauma and needs to recuperate."

I swallow several times before trying to speak. "Okay, thank you. I appreciate you taking the time to talk with me."

He gives me a small, professional smile. "Of course. If either of you need anything, there's a call button on the remote." He gestures to the bedrail. "Don't worry too much, Mrs. Sworr. Your husband is in great hands," Dr. Richmond adds before heading out.

Even through my thick sadness, flutters erupt at the mention of Rowen as my husband regardless of it not being true. I move the chair even closer until my knees brush the cool sheets. My puffy eyes flicker over every inch of him while my head tries making sense of all this. My brain is stuffed with the cotton of too much medical jargon but I definitely caught the part where he was stabbed—*multiple times*—and had an infection.

Who the hell would do something like this?

I keep staring at Rowen's motionless form, praying and wishing he wakes up soon. He needs to open his beautiful blue eyes and call me Sweetheart in that deep timbre I'm so crazy about. I need to feel the shivers coursing through my body from that sexy voice while being blasted with his beaming gaze.

Rowen is so still it's almost frightening, especially since I'm surrounded by the clinical white walls and antiseptic scent. Only the rhythmic rise and fall of his heavily bandaged chest lets me know he's alive, and I'm so effing thankful for that. I couldn't survive without him.

No freaking way.

Recalling every moment I wasted being cold and distant churns in my stomach like acid. I forfeited so much precious time by pushing him away and now, desperation to have every lost second claws at my aching spirit.

The doctor told me Rowen will be alright but I need to see him awake and well in order to believe it. My seeking gaze devours him and even in this battered state, he's the most gorgeous man

I've ever seen. His handsome features standout against the stark linens. Thicker scruff coats his jaw and the coarse hair scratches my fingers as I stroke along his golden skin. I lean in to kiss his warm cheek as a tear drips down my own. Wires and tubes are connected to his muscular arms as they relax against the bed, pumping necessary fluids into his veins but the sight is extremely upsetting to me. The large boulders in his biceps and sinewy veins in his forearms show his vitality, his amazing heath, yet he's strapped to machines. Beneath the gauze, I know there are slabs of rippling abs that make up an eight-pack.

How could this happen to him?

Only Rowen has the answers but it doesn't matter right now. This minute, I need to flood him with positivity and healing vibes. My hand slips into his and the familiar electricity zips through my body. Suddenly the monitor for his heart begins beeping wildly and my own pulse races at the thought of something being wrong. I clutch his palm tighter before placing a gentle kiss along his fingers, imagining my love flowing into him. The rapid noises slow to a regular beat and I release the nervous breath trapped in my lungs.

Rowen is going to be okay.

Even though he's unconscious and unaware of my presence, I can't yank my stare away. My body is drawn to his like a magnet that can't pull away. He'd appreciate my leering and maybe, somewhere deep inside of him, Rowen knows I'm here looking out for him. Carefully laying my head down near his hip, I imagine him combing through my hair and whispering sweet words of our forever. Tears distort my vision as a sob wracks through me. Rowen was suffering alone, bleeding out on the street, while I was talking nonsense with Willow. More time thrown away that I won't ever get back.

Please come back to me, Rowen.

Please, please, please.

A machine starts going nuts with loud sounds but before I can think much of it, the door slams open as an older couple storms in like gangbusters. My head whips off the bed as I spin in my chair. I blink quickly to clear the blur as my chest pounds in surprise. The woman is weeping and seems to be dragging the man behind her as they zoom up to Rowen's side. As the shock wears off and I study the pair in tense silence, there is a noticeable resemblance and I assume these are his parents.

Not wanting to draw unnecessary attention to myself, I remain quiet while they take in the scene before them. I'm sure they're going through similar waves of distress and need a minute to absorb it all. When the woman's sky-blue gaze swings my way, I'm certain she's Rowen's mother.

I can't seem to move, mostly because my hand refuses to let go of Rowen, so I give them a pathetic wave. "Hello. I'm Lark. Not sure if Rowen ever—"

His mother interrupts with a sweet smile. "Oh honey, we know who you are. Our son talks about you nonstop." She motions between them. "I'm Jean and this is Steve. We've been waiting by the phone for Rowen to call with some very exciting news. When we heard he was rushed to the hospital, that wasn't what we were expecting but drove over as quickly as we could. The nurse told us his wife was already here though . . ." Jean's explanation trails off while she blatantly peeks at my left hand.

My clouded mind is whirling as I try digesting her words. When they register, my face heats with extreme embarrassment. "Uhhh, yeah . . . about that." I stutter while figuring out what to say. My anxious gaze bounces along the sterile walls while I mentally smack myself for making up the lie.

Steve chuckles lightly at my obvious distress. "Don't worry, Lark. It will be official soon enough."

Jean shushes and shoots him a look while my heart trips over the meaning. Was Rowen actually going to—

"So, has the doctor been in yet? Do you know what happened?" His mother cuts into my thoughts.

I shake my head before nodding, realizing belatedly the mixed messages I'm sending off. My chin wobbles from the overwhelming onslaught of everything piling up.

"Yes, Dr. Richmond came by when I first arrived. When he was talking, I was still trying to wrap my head around the fact that Rowen was in the hospital. He was stabbed multiple times." I gesture to his chest as his mother claps a hand over her mouth. "And he has an infection. They had to operate too." A sobs breaks up my sentence and Jean wraps her arms around me. "I'm sure he'll be back soon to answer more questions," I manage to blubber out.

"Hush, dear. That's fine for now. He's going to be all right and you're here with him." She sniffles against my head. I lean into her, appreciating the motherly comfort, loving her already.

She steps back and clasps her husband's hand. Jean and Steve stand in silence while staring at their sleeping son. This seems like an intimate family moment that I'm intruding on but there's no separating me from Rowen. My weary eyes swing back to him as I give his hand a delicate squeeze.

His parents drag chairs to the other side of the bed before settling in. Lincoln comes in a while later, looking grief stricken and pale as hell, quickly explaining that the police took forever while getting his statement. We all talk together for a few hours until it's almost three o'clock in the morning with no change to Rowen's condition. Several nurses have stopped in and reassured us that he needs the rest and his body is working on healing. Jean and I openly share tears while Steve and Lincoln attempt to console us with lighter tales of Rowen's childhood. Even though this wasn't the ideal way to meet his parents, I'm so glad they're here.

When it's been made clear he'll keep sleeping for several more hours, his parents leave for a nearby hotel and encourage me to come with them. I politely decline, more than happy to remain exactly where I am. Even though Rowen isn't awake, he's here and that means this is where I'm meant to be. Lincoln takes off too, letting me know he'll be back in the morning.

My soul wants me to curl up on the mattress with Rowen but my brain takes stock of his injuries and the tangle of wires. Instead of causing more harm, I lay my head near his wounded middle and try relaxing my muddled mind.

Throughout the rest of the night, there are a few episodes where Rowen's blood pressure rises out of control as his heart rate soars through the roof. Nurses rush in to administer more medicine but before they do, I grasp his palm tighter and kiss his wrist. It seems like his pulse regulates from my touch alone but that's impossible. That's what I tell myself though and it helps steady my own frazzling system.

After the most recent scare fades away and the nurses shuffle out, I find a pen to make a change on my wrist that's long overdue. While glancing at my sleeping prince, I get the inspiration for a special design that we can share. After covering my empty heart with different ink and new meaning, Rowen gets his symbol of my unconditional love with a piece of the doodle. Fresh tears stream down the dried tracks from moments ago as I remember drawing similar pictures right before meeting Rowen. A small smile lifts my lips as I keep working through blurry eyes.

Eventually the pen stops and I manage to nod off because my body is too wrung out. Sleep cannot be denied any longer. Dreams of Rowen float through my subconscious. We're dancing on the porch at that cabin in Missouri, smiling and happy. Words of eternal love float around our swaying forms. He kisses my forehead before whispering sweetness in my ear. I snuggle closer and tell him this is forever.

The sensation of fingers softly stroking through my hair wakes me and a content sigh escapes my chapped lips. My eyes blink open and immediately lock onto Rowen's serene ocean gaze. A warm grin lifts his lips when he catches me awake.

"Hey, Sweetheart," he murmurs smoothly, in that husky voice I've been longing to hear.

Before Rowen can say anything else, I burst into uncontrollable tears as my heart sings with happiness.

TWENTY SIX

Rowen

When Lark starts crying, my immediate reaction is to console her but moving isn't easy. Shocks of intense pain ripple through me but the desire to hold her close roars above everything else. Without jostling my injured body too much, I reach my hand under her arm and pull lightly.

"Come here, Sweetheart. Lay with me," I breathe out while tugging again.

Lark sobs harder and snuggles into my hip but doesn't make a move onto the bed. Her head shakes back and forth before she manages to speak.

"I'm so happy you're all right. Oh my God, Rowen. I was so worried. *So, so scared.* Thank you for being okay," she sputters between hiccupped sniffles.

I yank on her harder and agony rips through my torso, sending blinding streaks of white through my vision as a brutal moan tears up my throat. Lark's face whips up as her flooded gaze scans my features.

"What's wrong, Rowen? Do you want me to call the nurse? Did I hurt you? Please don't fall back to sleep," she stammers as her trembling hand cups my jaw.

"What I need is for you to get your ass up here," I grind out through gritted teeth.

Lark bites her lip before standing on shaky legs. I lift my wired arm to make room as she gently settles in next to me, lying on her side and resting her head on my good shoulder. Feeling her weight causes the pain the cease and soothing peace washes through me. I kiss her hair and eagerly inhale the vanilla aroma lingering there. We both sigh as our bodies meld together.

"That wasn't so hard now, was it?" I ask against her temple, feeling tracks of tears drip down her face.

Her voice wobbles against my neck. "Fuck, Casper. I love you, so so much. And I missed you. This feels so good." She practically moans and my dick notices.

Good to know he's still working properly.

Now isn't the time for that.

"I love you too, Vix. Pretty sure I was dreaming of you but everything is a tad fuzzy. Was I out for long? I woke up a few minutes before you did. Not sure anyone else knows I'm back in the land of the living yet."

Lark looks at the clock before answering, "I think you were asleep for a little over twelve hours. After surgery, they gave you something that kept you under. I probably asked them a hundred times when you'd wake up. Pretty sure they stopped coming in here to avoid me," she mutters while placing her hand over my heart, as if making sure I'm really all right. I grasp her wrist and kiss her fingers before putting her palm back down.

"Figures I went under the knife with how I'm feeling," I say but quickly realize the mistake of bringing up my pain. When Lark pulls away slowly, her face is pinched with worry.

"Do you need something for the pain? We can call the nurse." Her voice is laced with panic. My chest clenches at her obvious concern.

My girl loves me.

A hum buzzes in my throat. "I love you, Sweetheart. Can we just lay here for a few more minutes before calling in the cavalry? You make me feel better just being here." My arm around her tightens until she eases back down.

"I love you so much, Row. So, so much," she mumbles and rubs her wet cheeks against me.

My spirit soars as a warm flush covers my skin. "Fuck, Sweetheart. That's the first time you called me Row You're giving me all the good stuff. Have you been holding out?"

"Nah, not on purpose. Maybe it just never felt right until now?" Her tone rises in question.

"It's perfect. Thank you for that." I release a heavy sigh. "Did they tell you more about what happened?"

Lark lifts her face until our eyes lock. "Lincoln found you unconscious behind a building downtown, in some alley. He told us you guys were there looking at a space for work. You were stabbed three times and got an infection. He feels pretty effing bad for leaving you. I think he almost cried. He'll probably be back soon with your parents."

"My parents were here?"

She giggles and says, "Yeah. Is that bad? You just tensed up real tight."

I can only think of how I included them in my plans and hope they didn't spoil anything.

"Of course it's not bad, Sweetheart. It would have been nice if I was conscious while you all met but whatever." I try to brush off my reaction before kissing her forehead.

Lark's smile drops when she asks, "Do you remember what happened?"

My gut clenches at the reminder of the fucking asshole and his knife. My body seems to tremble with fury as I recall what happened.

"Sounds like Linc already told you we were there for work. I was in a hurry to leave and pick you up so my mind was distracted. I was locking the door and getting ready to call you when a guy approached me. He wanted to rob me but didn't give me a chance before attacking. I tried fighting him off but his first cut was deep and fucked me up. I'm ashamed he beat me like that but what the hell could I do? I'm feeling pretty lucky at the moment, Sweetheart. I mean, you're here with me and I'm breathing."

Her eyes squeeze shut and a few tears spill down her face.

"It's my fault you're hurt," she utters almost silently while dipping her chin.

"No. Knock it off, Vix. Look at me." My tone is harsher than I intend. Lark glances up through lowered lids. "Don't say stupid shit like that. I'm alive because of you. There is no other reason for my heart to keep beating, Sweetheart. Don't ever say that stuff, all right? My blood boils thinking you're taking any blame." A few deep breaths help to rein in the frustration creeping up my spine. The longer I lay here, staring at Lark's stricken face, a calmness washes over me.

She's here. For me.

Lark's other arm lifts from between us so the new design on her wrist is visible. I gently clasp her hand before twisting it slightly as my foggy brain tries to catch up. She seems to notice my confusion and a tiny smirk dimples her cheek. Lark bites her lip while glancing between her skin and my stunned reaction.

"It's not permanent. At least not yet. It was time to cover up the emptiness though. I drew it earlier while thinking about us." She pauses for a deep breath. "You have the other part."

I immediately search my arm and find the spot along my left wrist where she gave me the same stamp. A blob of blue ink creates half a heart with a portion of an arrow sticking out from one side. When I scan Lark's tattoo again, realization clicks and my eyes get misty.

My pulse races and has the monitor next to me beeping wildly, but nothing can distract me from Lark's gesture. I bring our wrists together to make the design complete, like personalized puzzle pieces. The two halves form a full heart and the arrow acts like the connector between us. Separate it appears broken and wrong—the way my soul feels when she's not around. When we're linked, the meaning is clear. We belong together. Everything within me lights up like I've been set on fire, but these flames melt me into Lark forever. She did this for me. *For us.*

Serenity replaces any lingering madness as I envision last night the way it was supposed to be. My mind races as I begin planning all over again, suddenly rejuvenated with unstoppable strength thrumming through my muscles. Just as those thoughts begin taking root, aggravation slithers up my bandaged torso because I'm stuck in this hospital for the time being. As if hearing my silent complaints, a knock sounds before a woman pokes her head in the room. The nurse pushes the door open before waiting any longer and scowls our way.

What the hell is her issue?

Her focus seems to lock on my bedmate as she walks into the room. "Mrs. Sworr, you shouldn't be up there. You could cause serious damage." The nurse reprimands but my mind is stuck on the title she gave Lark.

"Oh my God," Lark mutters while burying her face in my neck. "This is *so* embarrassing. Why does this keeps happening?" Her voice is practically a squeak and I'm chuckling at her blushing cheeks.

When neither of us responds, the nurse pipes up again. "Clearly you're feeling better, Mr. Sworr. I take it your wife is the best type of medicine. How's your pain on a level from one to ten?" She questions from the bedside.

My wife. I love the sound of that.

I answer without taking my awestruck gaze off Lark. "I'm all good. A one or whatever is lowest. When can we leave?" Eagerness to complete my plans thrums through me like an electrical current, especially after hearing her addressed that way. My body burns like hell and I probably need something for the pain but my mind is occupied elsewhere for now.

"Mrs. Sworr is free to go whenever she likes. You on the other hand are stuck here for at least twenty-four hours," the nurse drones dryly.

Frustration is bubbling back to the surface.

"But I feel fine. Why do I have to stay?" I attempt to keep the growl out of my voice.

The nurse rolls her eyes while checking my chart. "Mr. Sworr, you had surgery and were running an extremely high fever. Not to mention the significant blood loss. It's hospital policy that you remain under a physician's care for at least twenty-four hours after such procedures. I'm sure a doctor will be in shortly to explain everything further. I suggest keeping the bed to yourself until then." She huffs before storming out.

I can't help but laugh at her retreating form. Lark isn't going anywhere. "Hey, Sweetheart. She's gone. Or should I call you Mrs. Sworr from now on?"

She groans loudly, her breath tickling my sensitive skin. "I told them we were married so they'd let me see you. They said immediate family only, Rowen. I wouldn't have done it otherwise." A deeper flush blooms on her face.

"I love it, Vix. A lot. Don't be shy about wanting to be my wife. You know I've been asking you." I can't help teasing her, especially when she gets all bashful. "Doesn't it have a nice ring to it?" Speaking of, that diamond better be in my pocket still. I'll have to check with Linc when he gets here.

Lark nudges me lightly. "Ask me right and we'll see." A beautiful smile tilts her luscious lips, which I gladly steal in a quick yet searing kiss.

We break apart before it gets too heated. Seems like we're in enough trouble here already.

"Making me work for it. I get it, Vix. I'll do right by you. Just wait and see."

"I have no doubt about it, Casper. You're always surprising me," she murmurs against my stubbled jaw.

I find the arrow charm resting against her neck and shift it slightly, thinking back to the day she captured my heart all those years ago. "Sweetheart, I am so damn glad you gave me another chance. You're the greatest thing that's ever happened to me. I can't wait to spend forever with you."

A shuddering breath wheezes past her lips. "Thank you for bringing love back to my life, Casper. I'm more than happy to admit you've pierced my heart."

My hand roams up and down her back before settling on her hip. "So, will you stay with me? Right here?"

"Me leaving is not even an option, Casper. You should know that."

My little vixen stealing my line from the night at her apartment causes my soul to overflow with gooey happiness.

Everything is going to be just fine.

TWENTY SEVEN

Lark

The last week has been tough but everything is finally getting back to normal. Rowen ended up spending two more nights at the hospital, which meant I stayed right there alongside him. He grumbled and groaned about being trapped in the sterile white room but I'd kiss his grumpy attitude away and snuggle deeper into his bulky embrace. When I'd hold our inked wrists together, a beaming smile would replace any hint of a scowl. Rowen really enjoyed our not-so-permanent tattoos, far more than I imagined and pure bliss squeezed my heart. The doctors told him there was nothing to complain about since his adoring wife was there, keeping him happy and occupied.

That lie bit me in the ass more times than I could count. Rowen ate it up too, making sure to point it out each time one of the medical staff referred to me as Mrs. Sworr. I would smile and blush like my skin was on fire, while the butterflies wreaked havoc on my belly.

Worst impulsive decision ever.

Okay, not really. It did get me into Rowen's room and allowed me to be with him constantly throughout his three-day stay. I enjoyed pretending to be his wife, probably too much, but it was easy to get whisked away in the fantasy. Once he was discharged, we took off without a backward glance but a pinch of disappointment hit me that our matrimonial farce was over. It evaporated almost immediately when Rowen asked me to be his stay-at-home nurse until he went back to work. I couldn't agree fast enough.

We've spent the last several days locked away from the world, sharing gentle kisses and soft touches. I've been testing out a lot of new recipes and am an expert at giving sponge baths. Rowen's been learning how to lay back and let someone else take care of everything for a change. His parents have been stopping by daily and are staying in town though the weekend. We've enjoyed plenty of laughs, mostly at Rowen's expense. Every moment has been great.

Well, except the afternoon we drove to the police station to identify Rowen's attacker. That sucked ass but they caught him and I gave him the finger through the mirrored glass. Immature but somehow rewarding, especially when Rowen enveloped me in a tight embrace and whispered how much he loved me. We shared a kiss and snuck back into our bubble of domesticated bliss.

Going to work today was unavoidable, especially for me due to a mandatory staff meeting this afternoon. It was my turn to groan and grumble but my sweet boyfriend swatted me on the ass before telling me he'd make up for our brief separation later. Rowen was planning to stop by his office for a few hours and check on some contracts. He promised it wouldn't be anything strenuous, just a few phone calls revolving around the partnership with that Brock guy from Texas.

The hours have thankfully flown by and it's almost quitting time. I used to be the last one to leave work, always consumed with paperwork and living for my job. Now, I can't seem to get out of here fast enough. As I'm packing up, my phone dings with a text notification.

Speaking of my reason to get home quickly . . .

Rowen: Change of plans, Vix. Meet me at the restaurant.

Suspicion tickles my brain because we always ride together.

Me: Why? I'm leaving work now. There's plenty of time before we're supposed to go.

It takes a few minutes for him to respond, which only escalates the annoying curiosity poking at me. Why is he being strange?

Rowen: Just because. I'm running behind schedule.

Me: That doesn't make any sense. It's only 5 and we aren't eating until 7.

Rowen: Vix, trust me. Just meet me there.

Urgh. Whatever.

I wasn't going to get into a texting battle with him. If Rowen wants to drive separate, we will. Rather than rushing home to an empty place, I spend an extra hour finishing up my daily notes and chatting with Willow. She brushes off my concern with Rowen and seems to think his behavior is totally normal. I'm not sure what's wrong with everyone today.

Is it Friday the 13th or something?

The evening only gets weirder as I pull into Brack's Box and find the parking lot completely empty. I try to call Rowen but get his voicemail. My finger jabs into the screen an excessive amount of times when asked to leave a message. I toss my phone away as frustration bubbles up my throat. Getting a drink—the stronger, the better—is exactly what needs to happen right now.

I practically sprint into the place with smoke steaming from my ears. After storming through the doors, my steps falter. Rowen is waiting behind the host stand, looking deliciously handsome as always. My wild gaze scans the lobby but there's not another person in sight. I'm on instant alert as my pulse takes off in a mad sprint.

What the hell?

Rowen breaks the silence. "Hey, Sweetheart." A wide grin spreads his gorgeous mouth and my knees almost buckle because of the dazzling sight. He chuckles at the stunned look covering my face.

"Thanks for coming to Brack's Box. Do you want a table or are you ordering out?" He asks while making his way toward my frozen form stuck in the entryway. My heart swells as he uses some of the first words I said to him all those years ago. I'm still fumbling for the answers to what all this means when he stops directly in front of me. But then it suddenly clicks together.

Is he going to . . .

My tone wobbles as a lump forms in my throat. "What's going on, Casper? Where is everyone?" Tears pool in my eyes when Rowen laces our hands together before pulling me closer.

"Do you believe in destiny? What about soul mates?" He murmurs while his nose lightly brushes up my jaw.

I manage to provide a breathy, *"Yes,"* while my legs threaten to fold under the weight of what's happening.

"I'm so happy to hear that because we're going back to the beginning, Sweetheart. Right here, at this podium where we first met, so we can rewrite history. From this day forward, every memory will be bright and beautiful, exactly the way it should have been. Just like our future will always be." He pauses and releases a heavy exhale. His blazing blue eyes beaming into my watery gaze.

"You wanted me to ask you the right way, but here's the thing, I'm not going to ask you, Vix. I won't ever give you the chance to refuse, but I will always give you exactly what you want." He takes a step back before getting down on one knee. My gasp is practically a scream as the tears start streaming down my cheeks in earnest.

"Marry me, Sweetheart. Say you'll truly be mine, forever and ever."

Rowen takes out a little velvet box and snaps it open. The sparking pink diamond almost blinds me as my heart stutters to a halt.

This is the exact experience I've always wanted, and of course Rowen gives it to me.

I'm nodding and holding out my trembling left hand while blindly wiping under my eyes with the other. That wicked sense of Déjà vu flashes through me like a high-voltage shock but this moment is brand new.

As Rowen slides the stunning ring on my shaking finger, I carefully collapse against him until we're in a heap on the floor. I'm showering kisses on every available piece of skin I find while whispering *I do* over and over again.

He laughs before capturing my lips and delivering a mind-melting kiss. Somewhere in between he growls quietly, "I'm glad you're already practicing for the wedding, Sweetheart."

EPILOGUE

Lark

The following weekend . . .

We rush down rows with flashing slot machines and spinning roulette wheels. The chandeliers are glittering overhead as we dash past groups of rowdy guys and scantily clad women. The chapel's double doors beckon us from across the crowded hallway as we race toward our spontaneous nuptials.

Well, let's be honest. We were planning this swift ceremony the second that engagement ring slid onto my finger.

Life is too short, right?

We already know that and the tragic truth behind those simple words rang even louder after Rowen was attacked.

Time is precious.

Cherish every moment.

Don't waste a second.

So, here we are. Diving into our future head first—together. Today we become husband and wife.

"Are you sure about this? Your parents won't be mad?" I

question belatedly as we scroll our signatures on the provided certificate, the bandages covering our fresh tattoos scratch along the paper.

Rowen chuckles before kissing my cheek. "Oh, they'll be furious but it's not their decision. I'm not waiting another minute for you to be my bride. The faster we can change your last name, the better."

I giggle against his scruffy jaw after giving him a noisy smooch; giddiness thrums through my body like an exotic beat.

"You're such a caveman and I effing love it."

"That's because I'm your caveman, Sweetheart," he murmurs along my lips.

Rowen is everything to me. My restoration in hope and faith. My belief in destiny and chance. My reason for being. My soul mate. My very own Prince Charming. My fairy tale brought to life and my happily ever after.

He's my soon-to-be husband.

The other half of my heart.

Short vows are exchanged while platinum bands are slipped over knuckles. Memories we will never forget pass by in a blur of tears and dopey smiles reflecting our pure bliss.

When the officiant announces, "You may now kiss your wife," an electrifying tremor passes through our connected hands.

Before my husband's lips descend to mine, Rowen mutters, "About damn time."

I couldn't agree more.

That first wedded kiss locks us into eternity, although our spirits seem to have bonded long ago.

We stumble out of the chapel clutching onto one another before being swallowed by the glitz and glam Vegas is known for. The fluorescent bulbs illuminating The Strip are extremely bright but my husband's elated face is the only sight for me. Rowen always steals the show.

"How about we get started on that fleet of lady-killer babies, Mrs. Sworr?" he seductively suggests before licking up my neck.

If I was wearing panties under this skin-tight sheath of white silk, they'd be incinerated from that comment alone. I lift a snarky brow while lacing our fingers together, metal clinks softly but the slight sensation feels like thunder along my skin.

"Lead the way, Mr. Sworr."

Looks like that meddling matchmaker really knew what he was doing after all.

The End!

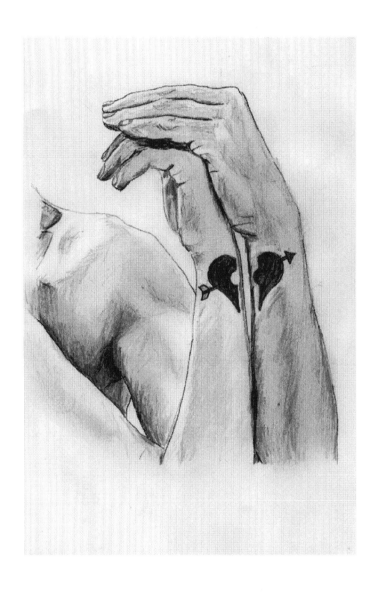

ACKNOWLEDGEMENTS

SINCE BECOMING AN author and publishing a novel, I've discovered that it truly takes a village . . . and my village continues to be mighty.

First and foremost, I need to thank my amazing husband—my real life Prince Charming and the reason I believe in true love again. When I told him I wanted to start writing books, he was nothing but supportive. For the past several months he's allowed me to binge on social media. He's patient when I ignore him for hours on end while I'm stuck in "the zone". Most importantly, he's the greatest father our little boy could ask for. Thank you so much, Honey Bunches.

My family didn't know I was writing books until Redefining Us released. Their reassuring responses were epic and they've been nothing but supportive. My sister, Kirs, is the artist responsible for creating the beautiful drawing of Lark and Rowen's tattoos. My brother-in-law helped me out with his medical knowledge. Even though my mom hasn't finished my first book, she cheers me on and believes in me.

Ace Gray needs a huge round of applause. Not only for editing my book but she also writes kick-ass novels. If you've never read her books, get on it. Ace is amazing and has become one of my closest friends. I am extremely thankful for everything she does, including showing me what words should never be used. Ever. You're the greatest, Ladyface!

My sister-from-another-mister, Chelle, has been my friend since elementary school and I'm very grateful for our friendship. Even when I'm stuck in a social media haze, she realizes how important this journey is for me. I'm so lucky to have her as my forever friend and don't know what I would do without her. I love you, MMM!

Talia from Talia's Book Covers is outstanding. I randomly stumbled upon an image from her page and an instant connection was formed. I appreciate your talent and patience daily. You are a lifesaver and I'm sending you a huge hug! Thank you for creating a stunning cover, as well as countless teasers and banners, for Rowen and Lark's story.

Cindy, you're an amazing person and I greatly appreciate all you do. Thank you for the daily messages that always make me smile!

Lauren Blakely and Kahlen Aymes brought romance back to my life many years ago. Your words inspire me daily and I will always cherish your friendships.

Ella James, you're the one I go to first because our brains work in very similar ways. Thank you for always understanding and calming my panic.

AM Hargrove is always ready with an answer to whatever question I whip up. She's a sunny spot on the darkest days, especially when she tells me the latest Walter story.

Thank you SO much Victoria Ashley, Penelope Ward, SL Scott, Sunniva Dee, Cora Brent, Adriana Locke, Tori Madison, J. Daniels, Beth Michele, Tia Louise, Winter Renshaw, Bella Love, M. Robinson, and many more for being so helpful with everything and anything. You're a spectacular group of ladies that I'm very lucky to consider friends. The author community is extremely supportive and I owe you all so much for continuing to encourage me.

To my reader group . . . the Hotties is my happy place and I enjoy our group so much. Thank you all for the love and happiness you bring!

JL Davis is the best motivator I could ask for. She keeps me writing when I'd rather be napping! Remember Nathan and Brittany from the neighboring cabin in the woods? They're the lead characters of JL's recent release Fight. Check it out!

I am very fortunate to be part of the #squadpod. Our little group is wonderful and I'm so thankful to be part of a troop!

A special note to my fellow besties: Jen, Bobbie, and Margie . . . I love you ladies!

A huge THANK YOU to Dawn from A Torrid Romance for always sharing and posting for me.

Crystal and Maggie, you two took a chance on a new author and I'm forever thankful. Your early reviews meant SO much to me. You were also the first to purchase signed copies of Redefining Us!

Hazel James, thank you for answering my military related questions. Your knowledge and experience was extremely helpful.

A huge thank you to my beta and proofreaders: Ace Gray, Cindy, Bobbie, and Jessica.

My formatting was done by Christine with Type A Formatting and she is amazing to work with. I owe her a lot for making my book look so pretty!

To my fellow bloggers, I know how hard you work for very little pay off. You make the author world go round so THANK YOU! I greatly appreciate each and every single one of you. I couldn't have done this without the support you all provide daily.

To the readers, you are the reason authors keep publishing their books. You are the life force behind this industry. You are simply spectacular. My gratitude to all of you runs very deep and I can't thank you enough for giving my novels a chance. Keep loving books for us, alright?

One last thank you to everyone that read Redefining Us and Forget You Not. I greatly appreciate it! Reviews are the fuel for a book's success so I hope you consider leaving one, especially if you loved these stories.

Thank you all so much!

ABOUT THE AUTHOR

H arloe was born and raised in Minnesota. She is married to an amazing man and they have an adorable baby boy. They are what make life worth living for her. Harloe has a day job that she loves and is also passionate about horses, blogging, country living, and having fun.

Harloe has been in love with romance since she was a little girl reading fairytales. The dream is to find the perfect person that completes your life, right? Novels have a way of bringing fantasy to reality and she's always up for an unforgettable adventure.

Stalk Harloe on her blog (insert link to word blog: harloe-rae. blog) or send her a message at *harloe.rae@gmail.com*

Made in the USA
Middletown, DE
30 August 2020

17450091R00132